**HIS ARMS WERE IMPRISONING HER,
HOLDING HER HELPLESS . . .**

His hands came down on her bare skin, his lips caught her mouth and held it. Those big hands of his slid across her flesh, stroking it, and his mouth was something that seemed to eat at her. She was lifted upward, and she began to tremble even as he was trembling.

She could hardly breathe. She felt her senses deserting her, all but the sensation of exquisite delight. And then something within her seemed to blossom outward, exploding . . .

More Romance from SIGNET

PORTRAIT OF LOVE

Lynna Cooper

A SIGNET BOOK
NEW AMERICAN LIBRARY
TIMES MIRROR

PUBLISHER'S NOTE

This novel is a work of fiction. Names, characters, places, and incidents are either the product of the author's imagination or are used fictitiously, and any resemblance to actual persons, living or dead, events, or locales is entirely coincidental.

Copyright © 1980 by Lynna Cooper

SIGNET TRADEMARK REG. U.S. PAT. OFF. AND FOREIGN COUNTRIES
REGISTERED TRADEMARK—MARCA REGISTRADA
HECHO EN CHICAGO, U.S.A.

SIGNET, SIGNET CLASSICS, MENTOR, PLUME, MERIDIAN AND NAL BOOKS are published by The New American Library, Inc., 1633 Broadway, New York, New York 10019

First Printing, November, 1980

1 2 3 4 5 6 7 8 9

PRINTED IN THE UNITED STATES OF AMERICA

1

She was setting out her paintings along the iron railing of Saint Louis Cathedral when she saw the man come to a stop, staring at her. He was on the opposite side of St. Peter Street, he was well dressed, he looked very much like a successful businessman. He stood there, motionless, and just stared at her.

Cherie Marsan sniffed and shrugged a shoulder. She was used to being stared at, her mirror in the little atelier-apartment she rented in Pirate's Alley told her she was beautiful. Ha! Right now, however, in this stained smock she was wearing, with her long golden hair hanging free under a cap, with all her oldest clothes on, she was far from being attractive.

So let him stare. Little good it would do him.

Cherie busied herself with the paintings she had carried here this day, to offer them for sale. Her business card was tacked to a board of drawings, showing her address to prospective buyers. The sun was warm, the air was pleasant, the visitors to New Orleans ought to be out in strength, wandering through the Vieux Carré. If she were lucky, she might even sell a painting or two.

A shadow touched the still life she had just hung. She turned, found herself staring up into a pair of intense black eyes. Cherie swallowed. This was the same man who had stopped to stare at her. She had not realized how handsome he was, with that deep bronze tan and that thick black hair. He had very white teeth, too, she realized, as he gave her a big smile.

"Five hundred dollars," he said softly.

Cherie blinked. "Wha-what?"

"I'll give you five hundred dollars."

An ugly suspicion slid into her mind. Cherie straightened abruptly. "What for?" she asked coldly.

"For a painting, naturally. What else?"

1

She wished he didn't have such a nice smile. It did things to her resolution to be standoffish. It was hard to be remote and unconcerned when he was beaming down at her in what appeared to be quite radiant happiness.

After a moment, she shook herself, realizing that she had been staring up at him just as intensely as he had been staring down at her—and grinning like a Cheshire cat. She touched her tongue to her lips and found they had become very dry.

Her hand lifted in a gesture. "Take any one of them," she murmured. "Take any two, for that matter."

He shook his head. "No, no. You don't understand. I want a painting of you. A self-portrait. I'll pay you five hundred dollars for it. Is it a deal?"

"You're crazy," she whispered.

He laughed full-throatedly, and despite her suspicions, Cherie could not help but like that laugh of his. When he sobered, he beamed down on her—like an adult humoring a small child, she thought angrily—and shook his head.

"No. I'm not crazy. I know very well what I'm doing. So how about it? You do a self-portrait of yourself for me, and I'll give you five hundred dollars. Fair enough?"

"Forget it," she snapped, and turned away.

"It doesn't have to be in oils. Even a simple pencil sketch would do. If I had a camera with me, I'd ask you to pose for a snapshot and still pay you the five hundred dollars."

He was smiling down at her as though he had offered her the Koh-i-noor diamond, free of charge. Cherie scowled. She had listened to propositions before from strange men. Always, naturally enough, she had turned them all down. At least, this one had an approach that was rather unique.

"No dice," she said flatly.

Out of the corners of her eyes, she watched him step back and run his eyes over her, then mutter under his breath. The guy was a nut! An absolute nut! He put both hands deep in his pockets and rocked back and forth on his feet, frowning slightly.

"Would you do me a favor?" he asked.

She glowered at him. "What favor?"

"Take off that godawful hat."

Cherie opened her lips to yell at him, then closed them. She knew what she looked like in that old thing she wore on her head. It was frayed and had a hole in it, but it was still the warmest hat she owned, and sometimes these spring days along the Mississippi River could get quite cold.

"For five dollars? For ten?" he asked plaintively. "Please?"

"Oh, for Pete's sake! There!"

She snatched off the hat, shook back her thick golden hair, and stared up at him. She was looking right in his eyes, she saw them study her very carefully, almost as though he were memorizing her face. To her surprise, he was not leering at her, as other men had done. He was considering her as an artist might do, before putting down her likeness on paper.

He nodded slowly, thoughtfully. Then he reached into his hip pocket and brought out a wallet. From the wallet he extracted a ten-dollar bill and handed it to her. Cherie looked at the bill suspiciously, asking, "What's that for?"

"We made a deal. The money's yours."

He smiled at her, and that smile was radiant. It did something to Cherie, it made her think that maybe she had misjudged this guy. Ha! She'd bet this was all part of his approach. The idea stiffened her spine.

"Keep your money. I don't want it."

His dark eyebrows lifted. "You're that rich?"

Cherie licked her lips. That ten dollars meant that she might eat well for a few days, if she were careful. After all, she hadn't sold a painting in over two weeks. Canvases and oils cost money, and if she were to make her living as an artist, she needed the tools of her trade.

He pushed the money toward her, extending his arm. "Go on, please. Take it. A bargain's a bargain."

"Look," she said angrily, "I don't quite get what it is you're trying to do. No amount of money is going to buy me, so if that's what's in your mind, keep your money and get lost."

She would swear that the look of surprise on his tanned face was genuine, and so was the distress that took its place. He shook his head at her and ran his hand through his thick black hair. She told herself that she would like to run her own fingers through his hair, and then grew angry at herself.

"The money is for what you did," he said slowly. "Just

taking off your hat. I'm very grateful. Maybe someday you may be grateful, too."

Cherie opened her eyes wide. He *was* a nut! Harmless, perhaps, but still a whacko. Hmmm. He didn't seem crazy, his eyes were very intelligent. And he was handsome.

"Okay, okay," she said, taking the ten spot in her fingers and folding it, then stuffing it into a pocket of her smock. "Thank you very much."

She just couldn't turn away, it wouldn't seem polite. "Anything else?" she wanted to know.

"I know you must think I'm crazy," he went on, "but I really will pay you five hundred dollars for a self-portrait. Just a head-and-shoulders job. That's all. Now how about it?"

Cherie frowned. "Why do you want it?"

There he went with that grin of his again. It was so friendly, so open, so—so honest, that she felt like a twerp getting angry at him. She shifted her position slightly, telling herself that five hundred dollars was more money than she could make in a month. Or even two or three months.

"It's a secret." He smiled. "I may be wrong, but—It could be very important. Important for you, that is. Now, don't ask me any more, I won't tell you anything other than that."

He certainly had a line. She wondered how many girl artists he had tempted—yes, and seduced!—with that spiel of his. It was a good one, she had to admit. Do a self-portrait for him, get five hundred bucks, and then one thing would lead to another and he would get her in bed with him. At least, that was the way it was supposed to work. But she was too smart for him.

"No painting," she said flatly. "At least, not of me. Any of these others I'll be more than happy to sell you."

He shook his head. "They're very good, all of them. Probably worth their weight in gold, even with gold the price it is. But no, thanks. I don't have any use for them. It's your picture I want."

Some of her artist friends had drawn a little nearer, she noted, wondering, no doubt, if she were having trouble. Cherie shook her head at them, silently assuring them that she needed no help.

"Sorry," she said softly, not wanting to hurt the guy. "I can't do that."

He sighed and reached for his wallet again. This time he drew out a card and handed it to her. Cherie stared up at him a moment, then dropped her eyes to the pasteboard.

BRIAN CUTLER
Attorney-at-law

A lawyer. Now why in the world would a lawyer want her self-portrait? Or maybe he wasn't a lawyer at all, but just posing as one to add to the mystery. Cherie began to feel a little out of her depth.

"If you change your mind, please get in touch with me." He smiled down at her. "The offer still goes, you know. It's possible I may even go as high as a thousand dollars for that picture."

Her mouth went dry. A thousand dollars, just for a self-portrait! Ha! Maybe she was the nut, not him. That much money would make her almost independent. But she was still very suspicious of him.

"I'll think it over," she muttered.

He nodded at her, still smiling, his eyes going over her face, business card and her too, as though he were memorizing them. Cherie told herself she ought to feel flattered. She was pretty enough, almost beautiful, she supposed, when she put her mind to looking attractive.

"I'm going to keep pestering you until you agree." He chuckled. "Remember that. Oh, yes. If you change your mind, just give me a ring at my office and I'll get over to see you fast."

He waved a hand, turned on a heel, and walked away. Cherie stared after him, wondering who in the world he really was and what he really wanted with her. Well, she knew what he wanted with her, of course. Just what any other red-blooded man would want.

"Fat chance," she grumbled as she turned back to her paintings.

A man with a thick beard came to her side. He was one of the artists who shared the cathedral railings with her. "What was that all about?"

Cherie said, "I think I was just propositioned, but I'm not sure. He offered me a thousand dollars to do a self-portrait for him."

"And you turned him *down*?"

Cherie grinned. "I'm crazy, hey?"

"Honey, you are. You positively are!"

Cherie stared up the street along which Brian Cutler had just moved. Inside herself, she felt suddenly empty. "Maybe I am, Chuck. Maybe I am."

Chuck Peters walked away, shaking his head. Cherie turned back to her paintings, began to arrange them more carefully on the iron railings. Was she crazy? A thousand dollars was more money than she had ever had in her life. What if he were trying to seduce her, get her into bed with him. She could always say no, couldn't she? He did not seem the sort of person who would fight with her, try to overcome her physically.

She sighed and settled herself to spend the day trying to sell one of her oils. Despite her intent, her thoughts kept wandering away from the people who came to stare at the paintings. She kept seeing Brian Cutler's tanned face and that pleasant grin. Nobody that nice could be as bad as she was suspecting him of being.

Maybe *she* was the nut. A thousand dollars, and she had said no.

"Phooey," she muttered.

The day dragged by slowly, and Cherie rested on her little campstool in the sun. Men and women came and stared, they admired her paintings, some of them even enthused, but nobody bought any of them. After a time Cherie just sat there and let them look. She did not even offer to reduce her prices.

She ate her sandwich, which she had made in her atelier-apartment, and drank chilled milk from a thermos bottle. She watched the shadows lengthen along the street. Soon it would be time to pack up her paintings and go home.

It was while she was gathering her oils that she noticed the heavyset man who had been ambling almost lazily down the street. She was lifting one of the larger of her paintings, about to put it in the case with the others, when she looked up and saw the man come to a complete stop and stare hard at her. His face had been friendly enough while he had been walking; now it seemed to harden even as she stared. Then he gave her a look of almost malignant dislike.

Cherie swallowed. What was the matter with her? Why should that man stare at her in such obvious hate? Her fingers loosened, she almost dropped the painting she was holding. As she bent to retrieve it, the man swung about on a heel and went back up St. Peter Street almost at a trot.

She stared after him, nonplussed. What was wrong with the guy? Sure, she was wearing old clothes, but she wasn't as horrible-looking as all that, was she? The guy acted as though he'd seen a ghost. Cherie stuffed her painting in with the others almost angrily.

This had been some day, all right. First that kook who wanted to give her a fortune for her portrait, then this idiot who acted as though she'd killed his best friend. Oh, well. There were days like that, she supposed.

Carrying her paintings, she trudged toward Royal Street. As she walked, she thought about what she might have for dinner. There was some stew left, but she had eaten stew for five or six days running now. Eggs, of course—she always had those, she could whip up a mixture of eggs with tomatoes and onions. A little wine might go nice with eggs.

Cherie made a face. She really didn't feel like eggs, she wanted something more substantial—say, a nice steak. The only trouble with that was, steaks cost a lot of money. But wait! She had ten whole dollars, didn't she? Sure. That lawyer (if he was a lawyer) had given it to her for taking off her hat.

She laughed out loud. "That was the smartest thing I ever did, letting him look at my hair. It will feed me for a couple of nights."

Her steps grew lighter, she almost danced as she walked. She knew just where she could get the kind of steak she wanted. As she moved along, she began to sing very softly, almost under her breath.

With a thick steak and a bottle of red wine under an armpit, she walked toward Bourbon Street. Soon now, she would be indulging in a quick shower, she would let the wine breathe while she was doing that, and then she would cook the steak. Her mouth began to water.

Sometimes at night when she had come home from the cathedral railings, she painted. But not tonight. She didn't want to paint, not now. She just wanted to indulge herself, eat a good meal, and maybe even finish half the wine bottle. The Chianti would make her drowsy and she would get a good sleep. Maybe she would even dream of spending that thousand dollars.

Cherie giggled. First she had to paint herself down on

canvas before she could get all that money. But why not?
So the guy wanted a portrait of her. So she might even
paint it.

As she turned to enter the hallway of her apartment,
she threw a glance back down the street. Cherie paused.
Was she mistaken, or was that the same heavyset man she
had seen earlier, standing there at the corner and staring
at her? A feeling of uneasiness touched her, and she
paused to regard him more closely. But even as she did,
the man swung about and trotted off.

She shrugged. Maybe it was, maybe it wasn't. It made
no difference to her. She unlocked the street door and
stepped into the inner courtyard of the house she shared
with other artists, with other young people who worked in
the Vieux Carré. Moving across the courtyard with its
huge stoneware basins that held plants and flowers, she
caught the smell of frying onions. Hmmm. Might be a
good idea to fry some onions herself, they always went
good with steak.

Once in her apartment, which consisted of a big room
with a smaller room off to one side that formed a kitchen,
she placed her paintings against a wall, then snatched off
her hat and tossed it. She bent then and touched a match
to the little gas heater. She undressed, walking toward the
little bathroom, and when she was inside it, turned on the
shower water. By the time she had showered, the room
would be pleasantly warm. The water was hot, so she reg-
ulated it, then stepped under it, reaching for a bar of soap.

After a few minutes, she toweled herself off and
wriggled into her pajamas, then into a woolen robe. Her
feet she slid into thick slippers. Then she went to get the
steak.

In moments, the smell of frying onions made her mouth
water. She put in the steak and watched as it began to
sizzle. From moment to moment she lifted the steak with a
fork, turning it, making certain it was cooked all over.
Then she transferred the steak to a platter and went to
fetch the Chianti.

Cherie ate slowly, enjoying the taste of the meat, of the
wine. It had been a long time since she had enjoyed such a
meal. She lingered over the wine when the meat was gone,
rolling the Chianti about on her tongue, reveling in the
luxury. As she did, she thought some more about Brian
Cutler.

She still had change left from the ten spot he had paid her. Two or three dollars, anyhow. She could buy another steak tomorrow, if she wanted. A smaller one, perhaps, but still, a steak. And she would have enough wine left to sip with it.

A thousand dollars will buy an awful lot of steak and wine, Cherie, she told herself. You really are a ninny not to call up the guy and promise to do that portrait for him. So what if the guy's a kook? A thousand dollars in your handbag will fit just as neatly as it does in his wallet.

If she had a phone, she would call him right now. She would! She had been stupid to refuse him earlier. Tomorrow she would call him. If the guy wanted to waste his money, who was she to object?

She cleaned up, washing the dishes and the wineglass after she had put away the half-filled bottle of wine. She took her time, there was no hurry. Tonight she was going to get into bed and read a novel. She had half a dozen paperbacks on a shelf, unread.

It was warm and cozy under the bedclothes. Cherie snuggled herself against a couple of pillows propped to the headboard, and opened the book she had selected. In moments, she was into the book, enjoying the problems of the heroine.

She read for about an hour, then began to feel too warm. Slipping out from under the blankets, she ran to the gas heater, turned it off. In a little while, she knew from past experience, the room would grow cool and make for good sleeping. With a sigh, she got back into the bed and pulled the covers up about her.

Cherie read on until her eyelids began to feel heavy. It was pleasant here, with the room growing colder, with the blankets up about her. Just a couple more pages, then she would be so tired, she knew she would sleep well.

She tossed the book aside, with a marker in it, then reached for the light switch. The room darkened instantly, just a trace of moonlight filtered in through the window. Cherie snuggled down under the covers. She would get a good night's sleep, tomorrow she would think some more about doing that self-portrait. After all, a thousand dollars was nothing to sneeze at. . . .

She dreamed vividly, as she always did. In her dream, she had painted a very lovely landscape with lush green meadows and rows of beautiful trees. The picture was so graphic that she stood and stared at it, entranced. And as she stared, she seemed to see a—something—that was in that painting, but that she could not recall having put into it.

She leaned closer, staring at the thing that was far off, back there where she had oiled in a little brook, in the background. As she stared, the thing grew larger, and she recognized it for a walking man.

It can't be! she told herself. I didn't paint in a man!

The walking man grew larger, larger. With a muffled cry of surprise, she recognized the man as Brian Cutler. Now, what in the world was Brian Cutler doing in one of her paintings? She definitely had not oiled him in! Eyes wide, she watched him come walking toward her. As he came nearer, she saw that his face was smiling at her, as though in welcome.

Larger and larger he grew, until it seemed he would step off the canvas and stand before her. Now he was reaching out a hand and the hand was emerging from the painting to clutch at her shoulder.

She was being shaken.

"Stop it, stop it," she cried. "You aren't real. You can't be."

The shaking went on and on. . . .

Her eyelids lifted. Brian Cutler was bending over her, calling her name, clinging to her shoulders with both hands, and his face was terribly frightened.

"Cherie! Cherie! Wake up, wake up!"

She could not move. There was something very wrong with her. Only her eyes seemed to be alive as they looked up into his face. She wanted to ask him what he was doing here in her room, in the middle of the night, and could not.

He muttered under his breath, then slid his arms under her body. Like that, he lifted her and her blankets from the bed. He began to carry her toward the door of her little atelier-apartment. Cherie could not resist him. Her muscles seemed turned to water. Her head hung back over his arm and her legs dangled.

What in the world was the matter with her?

Or—was she still dreaming?

2

He carried her out onto the balcony and set her down. The outdoor air was cold, penetrating. But the blankets were wrapped about her and his arms clung to her, holding her to him. Her head fell forward against his chest.

"Were you trying to kill yourself?" he grated.

For a moment, Cherie could not understand him. Kill herself? Now whatever gave him that idea? She tried to form words with her tongue, but her tongue would not obey her. Instead, she shook her head.

"Don't," she managed to mumble. "Don't know what ... you're talking about."

He looked down at her in the moonlight, and it seemed to Cherie, even as she forced herself to look up at him— her head was so heavy, her neck so weak!—that there was a touch of horror in his eyes. The horror faded into deep concern, into something like pity.

"The gas," he said softly.

Cherie blinked at him. "What gas?"

"Here, walk around," he murmured.

She didn't want to walk, she was too lethargic. But his arm about her turned her, guided her. She took a few steps along the narrow balcony, then a few more.

"Breathe deeply," he ordered. "Go on, breathe!"

"I'm breathing. If I didn't, I wouldn't be alive."

She began to giggle helplessly. He was so funny. Telling her to breathe, indeed. But she took a few breaths, and as she did, her head began to clear. It was easier to walk now. No longer need she lean against him with his arm about her to support her.

And yet, she liked the feel of that arm about her, helping her, guiding her. She walked more firmly now, she breathed more deeply.

Then she stood stock-still. Oh, my God! She thought. Suppose the neighbors should see me like this, in my pajamas! With a man, yet. Walking up and down on the balcony in front of my little apartment. What would they say?

She turned in his arm and stared up at him. "Wha-what are you doing here?"

"Never mind that. Just be damn glad I came."

"But—but—"

He turned her, bringing her in against him so he could put both arms around her and hold her against him. Cherie felt her heart begin to pound a little faster. If the neighbors saw her now, they would be certain she was having an affair.

Ha! That would be the day.

She found words. "What in the world is going on?"

His face lost its tender look, grew very grim. "You tried to kill yourself."

Cherie opened her mouth and forgot to close it. Numbly she kept staring up at him, indignation rising inside her like a tidal wave. Her eyes grew big, and she stuttered as she sought to reply to him.

"I d-did n-not! I w-went to bed and was a-a-asleep when you came barging in!"

"Sure you were. You were so asleep that in another hour you would have been dead. That's how much asleep you were."

"What are you—" Her voice broke and she had to fight to assume control over it. As calmly as she could, she asked, "What are you trying to say?"

His eyes glared down at her, furious. Instead of answering, he turned her, marched her back to the door of her room, which she saw now had been broken open.

"Smell!" he grated.

She sniffed and began to cough. Hurriedly, he backed her away from the open doorway, held her tightly.

"Gas," she mumbled.

"Right the first time. From your gas heater. Of all the dumb things to do, turn it on and forget to light it. Or"—and here his voice grew hard—"did you do it deliberately?"

She stared into his eyes, with fright moving coldly all through her body. Cherie shivered despite the blankets and his arms, which held her. In a small voice, she whispered, "I shut off the gas. I did. I remember it quite well. Oh, I had the heater on earlier, but before I went to sleep I got out of bed and turned it off."

He was looking down at her, and there was sympathy and worry in his gaze. "Okay, then. I believe you. But if you didn't turn on the gas—who did?"

A terrible thought slid into her head. She fought against it, but some perverse imp made her say in a small voice, "You could have."

Brian opened his mouth, closed it. His arms fell away from her so suddenly that she teetered backward. Instantly his arms came out to grab her again, bringing her up against him.

"I ought to turn around and march out of here," he snapped. "Is that all the thanks I get for saving your life? To be accused of having tried to kill you?"

Cherie mumbled. "Well, I didn't really mean it. There would be no sense in your turning on the gas, then rescuing me, I guess."

"For your information, I came here to talk you into doing that picture of yourself. A lucky thing I did, too. If I hadn't, you'd have been dead by now."

She shivered. "Who could have done it?"

He eyed her closely. "Got any enemies? Anybody who doesn't like you? As a person? As an artist?"

She shook her head. She made friends easily, she kept her friends. There was no one she could think of who . . .

She gasped, "That man!"

"What man?"

She told him about the heavyset man who had been staring at her, who had apparently followed her home. Brian listened, head to one side, his eyes intent on her face. As she went on talking, Cherie felt her nervousness fall away. Was it because she had someone to share her fears, her worries? Or was it simply because it was Brian Cutler standing with her, listening so intently?

When she was done, Brian nodded. "It could be. Though why he would want to kill you is beyond—"

He broke off, staring into space above her head. Cherie watched his eyes closely, she was positive that he had thought of a reason why someone would want her dead. "Well?" she asked anxiously. "What are you thinking?"

His eyes returned to her, and he smiled. "I'm thinking I'd better take you away from here, first of all. Let's go back inside—the gas ought to have dissipated by this time—and pack a bag."

Cherie stirred. "Pack a bag? What for?"

"You don't think I'm going to let you stay here any longer, do you? You'd be a sitting duck for a repeat performance. That man could come back tomorrow night, or the night after, or even some night next week when you'd have relaxed your guard, and do it all over again."

She spread her hands. "I can't walk away. I have to paint, to earn a living."

"Don't be silly. If you're dead, you won't be able to earn a penny. As far as painting goes, you could paint where I'm going to take you."

She turned and stared at the open door of her room. Suddenly she did not want to go back into that room. Most positively, she did not want to sleep in there, not anymore. Her familiar little room would be like a death trap. Cherie began to shiver.

His hands were gentle as they turned her. "Come on, pack some clothes. My car is out on the street. We can be away from here in a few minutes."

"We-ell, if you think I should . . ."

An arm about her waist propelled her toward the door. She hesitated at the edge, but he was beside her, and as she sniffed, she realized the strong smell of gas had abated. Cherie walked into her room and, sliding out of the blankets, tossed them onto the bed.

She realized that all she had on were her old pajamas. They fitted her pretty closely, too. Cherie gasped and ran for the bathroom, closing the door behind her. She turned on the light, stared at her reflection in the mirror.

Hmmm. The pajamas were even thinner than she had thought. Brian Cutler must have gotten an eyeful when she slid out of those blankets! Her face was flushed, her eyes bright. Relax, Cherie. All he could have done was look. Still! She didn't like the idea of being almost naked in her thin pajamas with Brian Cutler around.

Or—did she?

"Phooey on that," she muttered. "I must be losing my grip."

"What's that? What did you say?"

That was Brian on the other side of the door. Cherie yelled, "Nothing. Just talking to myself."

There was a pause, then he said, "Don't you need some

clothes? I see your slacks and sweater out here, along with some—er—bits of underwear."

Cherie mumbled under her breath. Then she put a hand on the bathroom doorknob and yelled, "Look the other way. I'm coming out."

She opened the door, peeped into her bedroom. Brian was standing with his back to her, teetering back and forth, hands in his trouser pockets. Cherie guessed it was safe enough to run out and snatch up her clothes. She sprang into the room, ran to the chair where she had placed her slacks and sweater, and snatched them up. As she did, she flashed a glance at him. He was still standing with his back to her, staring at the wall. She turned and marched back into the bathroom, but as she was closing the door, she remembered that there was a mirror on the wall at which he had been looking. The mirror was so positioned that if he were looking into it, he could see her quite clearly.

"A voyeur," she muttered. "That's what he is."

But no matter what she called him, she could not deny the little thrill of pleasure that ran through her. She was female enough to want to be admired, and she imagined that the sight of her in these pajamas might be very interesting to a man.

Cherie sneered and began slipping out of her pajamas.

When she was dressed, she gave a last look into the bathroom mirror. Her long yellow hair fell in smooth waves to her shoulders and below, and her face seemed filled with color. She nibbled at her lips. To make them redder? She told herself not to be silly. She couldn't care less about Brian Cutler. Well, as a man, of course. Naturally, she was grateful to him for rescuing her from her gas-filled room.

She moved out into the bedroom, aware that he was sitting at the kitchen table. Cherie wondered if she ought to offer him a cup of coffee, then decided against it. She wasn't lighting anything in this room for a long time to come.

There was a big, battered old valise under her bed. She pulled it out and began filling it with clothes. Rather ruefully, she reflected that she did not have very many good clothes. Almost shamefacedly, she hid some of them from his eyes as she thrust them into the bag.

She paused and took a look around. There were other

things she would want to take with her, but not right now. All she needed at the moment was clothes.

Then Brian was beside her, reaching for the valise. "All set?"

"I-I guess so."

His hand caught her elbow, brought her with him to the door.

Cherie ran her eyes over the door, rather ruefully. She said, "I've been meaning to get a better lock. I just kept putting it off."

Brian chuckled. "All I had to do to open it was give a good shove and turn the knob. I rather imagine that was how your would-be killer got in, too. Though I suppose he had a set of skeleton keys in his pocket, just to make sure."

Cherie shivered. "Don't talk like that. It's scary."

"Better to talk about it and be safe. If you ever go back there, the first thing we've got to do is get a locksmith in to make that door impregnable."

She glanced at him. "We?"

His grin was wide. "Sure, we. You don't think I'm going to lose you, now that I've saved your life, do you?"

They went down the circular staircase to the courtyard. In all the time she had lived here, Cherie had always loved that courtyard, with its huge, potted plants, its several staircases, its balconies. There was romance about such a place, she could imagine a carriage with horses waiting for the people who had lived here a century or more ago, people who had used the whole house for their family and servants. Or slaves. Often enough, she used to dream about that other time and what the people who had lived here were like.

As they went swiftly across the big flat stones that surfaced the yard, she said, "You never told me what you were doing here. How come you were on hand to save me?"

He chuckled softly. "I was driving through the city when I decided to visit you."

"At two o'clock in the morning?" she asked, incredulous.

"Sure. Why not? I figured you might not put up too much of a fight at that time of morning. I want that self-portrait, Cherie. I want it very desperately."

At the street door, she turned to face him. It was dark here, there was light only from a small electric light bulb inside a glass shield. By its dim light, his face seemed almost nebulous.

"You are crazy," she muttered.

"Lucky for you I am."

Well, she had to agree to that, of course. If he hadn't come here tonight— But she made herself ignore that thought. Instead, she forced herself to stick to the main issue.

"Well? Why did you? Come to visit me, that is."

"To beg you to do that self-portrait." His voice changed, became almost argumentative. "What's the big deal, anyhow? Why shouldn't you do a self-portrait? Lots of artists have done them. Why should you be the exception? Especially when I'm willing to pay you good money for it?"

There was no reason, really. Except her stubbornness, of course. She was a girl who liked to have a good reason for everything she did. She watched as he opened the street door, then she stepped out on the sidewalk. He came after her, carrying her valise.

The street was empty save for a Ford Granada. Cherie glanced from the car to Brian. "That yours?"

"It is. Wait, I'll unlock the door."

He opened the door, held it as she slid inside. Then he carried her bag around to the trunk. In moments he was beside her in the front seat, sliding the ignition key into its slot. The motor came to life, purred.

He pulled away from the curb with Cherie watching his face. He drove easily, competently. She wondered if he did all things as expertly.

"Where are we going?" she asked as they swung onto Burgundy Street.

"To River View. That's my home."

"Oh?"

Brian grinned as he glanced at her. "Will you relax? Nobody's going to seduce you. You'll be safe there as you'd be in your own place." He hesitated a moment, then added, "Safer, as a matter of fact. Nobody's going to come busting in on you there."

Not even you?

Cherie decided she had better keep that thought to herself.

She settled herself comfortably, crossing her legs, wondering as she did so if she were doing the right thing. Here she was, going off in the nighttime to a place she didn't know, with an almost complete stranger beside her. Of course, he might be telling the truth: maybe he really was a lawyer, maybe he did have her best interests at heart. On the other hand, all this might be an elaborate ploy to get her off somewhere alone where she would be completely at his mercy.

Her eyes drifted toward his face. He did not look like a villain, she had to admit. She could not imagine any reason why he would want to go to such elaborate lengths to kidnap her, if that was what was in his mind. She had no money to pay a ransom. And if he were trying to seduce her, he sure was going to a lot of trouble for nothing.

"Come on," she found herself saying, "What's the angle?"

He glanced at her. "Angle? What do you mean?"

"Why are you doing all this, getting me off with you, away from my apartment?"

Brian stopped the car, braking it. There were no other cars about, they were all alone at the moment on the road. He turned and faced her, frowning.

"I'm trying to save your life," he said quietly. "Can you get that through your pretty head? Just saving your life, that's all."

"And who would want to kill me?"

He hesitated. "I'm not sure—though I have a pretty good idea."

"You've got to be kidding!" Cherie sat up straight in her amazement, eyes wide and lips parted. "Do you mean to tell me you know somebody who might want me dead?"

"I sure do."

She gaped at him. For an instant she thought he might be crazy, really crazy. A lunatic, obviously insane. But as she stared into his eyes, she knew very well that whatever else he might be, Brian Cutler was not nuts. He was cold sober, and highly intelligent.

And yet . . .

Rather weakly, she said, "Hey, hold on. Do I get you right? There *is* somebody who wants me dead? You mean that honestly?"

"I most certainly do."

"But why? Why?"

He shook his head. "I can't tell you. Not yet."

Cherie blinked. This guy was out of his skull. She was

of half a mind to open the car door and step out. But that would be stupid. Obviously, Brian Cutler knew something that she didn't know, and that it was imperative for her to learn, for her own safety. If he were telling the truth, that is. But what in the world could he know?

I've got to calm down. No sense in getting uptight about all this. Sooner or later he's got to tell me. So why not sooner?

She slid a little closer to him on the car seat. Her hand came up to touch his tie, straighten it. "Oh, come on, Brian. You can tell me. Please?"

His eyes grew tender as they looked down at her, but he shook his head. "I can't. Not yet. There's something I have to show you first. Otherwise"—and here he grinned like a little boy—"you'll think I've flipped my lid."

She thought that already—or almost, she decided. But her hand left his tie to caress his jaw. "Pretty please?"

Brian Cutler sighed. "I can see I'm not going to get any rest until you know what I know. But I have to tell you all in good time. Look. I'm running this show. Let me do it my way. How about it?"

Cherie clenched her teeth. She had never before bothered to try and wheedle information out of any man. Always, she had looked down her nose at females who had used their sex to get men to do what they wanted them to do. She had felt it demeaning.

Ha! But now . . .

She slid even closer so that her thigh was against his, and she was almost touching him with her breasts. She lifted one arm and put it about his neck.

"Why won't you tell me?" she whispered, hoping she was making it sound seductive.

"Because I want you alive."

"Is it so dangerous, this secret of yours?"

"It sure as hell is, to you."

She could have slapped him. Fury rose inside her that she had to fight against. He was the most exasperating man she had ever known! She wanted to rant and rave at him.

Instead, she found herself saying sweetly, "I wish I could believe you, Brian. But there's nothing in my life that is as dangerous as you make out your secret to be."

"Oh, yes, there is."

She slid closer, and both her arms were around his

neck. Up this close, she was positive that he was aware of her femininity. He had to be made out of wood, not to be. She despised herself for what she was doing, but it was the only thing she could think of to learn what it was he knew and she didn't.

"What, Brian? What's so dangerous about me? Why would anyone want to kill me? I'm just an unknown artist, a nobody."

"Oh, no, you're not."

"How's that again?"

His face was very close to hers. If he leaned forward just a little more than an inch, he would be kissing her. Cherie found that her heart was pounding faster and faster. Or was that his heart banging away in echo to her own?

"I said you're not just an unknown artist. Not really."

"I'm not?"

Surprise held her against him, unable to move. Vaguely she was aware that he had put his arms about her and was holding her rather tightly. As a matter of fact, he was crushing her against him. The funny part of it was, she wasn't trying to get away.

"No, you're not."

Almost dreamily, she murmured. "Okay, then. I'm not really Cherie Marsan. Is that what you're trying to say?"

"Mmmmm-hmmmm."

"Then who am I?"

His grin was impish. "Can't tell you. Not yet."

"Why not?"

"You going to stop asking me questions?"

There was something in his voice that should have warned her. But she was not thinking very well right then, not with his arms holding her, with their lips so close.

"No, I'm not going to stop," she breathed.

"Okay, then."

His arms tightened. He swept her up against him until she could hardly breathe. And then he kissed her.

3

The kiss went on for quite a time. Later, Cherie was to tell herself that Brian was something of a monster to take advantage of her this way. But at the moment, all she could do was cling to him and kiss him just as furiously as he was kissing her.

Sensations the like of which she had never experienced ran helter-skelter through her. Her heart raced wildly, there was a weakness all through her body; she could not have moved to save her life. Her breasts swelled, her every nerve end tingled delightfully. She wanted this kiss to go on and on. She wanted to forget the whole world, she needed to exist only to know this strange madness.

In time, she came to her senses. Her hands pushed him back and away, and she stared down deep into his eyes. Well, maybe that was a mistake, to look into his eyes, because all she could see in them was tenderness and deep affection.

Words stuttered on her tongue, but she could not voice them. There was indignation in her, but over that was a layer of excitement, of happiness, that she could not explain.

Finally she gasped, "You have some nerve!"

To her amazement, he was very contrite. "You're right. I'm sorry. I should never have done that. It's unforgivable."

He didn't have to be so abject about it, she thought wildly. After all, it was only a kiss. Just the same . . .

"Why did you? Why did you kiss me?" she pressed, aware that his arms had fallen away from her and that she felt cold and shivery now where they had been holding her.

Brian stared off down the empty street. He shook his head. "I lost control. I have no other excuse to offer." He hesitated, then added, "If you'd rather I took you to a hotel instead of to my home, I'll do it."

They sat apart now, Cherie regarding him from the corners of her eyes. The excitement was still in her blood, in her flesh, but over it was a feeling that she must not lose contact with this man, that there might even be something very special about him.

"I have no money to waste on hotel rooms. You'd better take me with you. Besides, if someone wants me dead, wouldn't they check into the hotels to see if I were staying there?"

Eagerly he agreed. "That's true. You'd be far safer at River View."

He started the engine, began once again to drive through the night. Cherie sat quietly beside him, lost in her thoughts, savoring the reactions of her body. Forgotten were the questions with which she had been bombarding him. All she could think about was that kiss and what it had done to her.

She glanced at him. Had he felt the same way she had?

"I suppose you go around kissing girls all the time," she found herself saying, almost angrily.

"As a matter of fact, I don't. I can't recall the last girl I kissed."

"Oh, no?"

"I've been too busy establishing a law practice to bother very much about girls. It takes time to get a practice together, you know. I've done pretty well, all things considered. But I haven't had time for girls."

Why was she so delighted to hear that? It could make no difference to her whether Brian Cutler went around kissing a dozen girls a day. No way. Still, there was a little part of her that rejoiced to hear him say what he had. Cherie hugged herself and sat very still, dreaming.

Suddenly she sat up straight. "Hey! Are you married?"

"Of course not. Don't have time to be married."

Cherie smiled to herself, sinking back against the car seat.

She paid little attention to where the car was going. Except that after a time she grew aware that they were on a lonely road, with stately oaks on either side. In the distance she could see the gleam of moonlight on the waters of the Mississippi. Her eyes went this way and that, studying the land past which they moved.

Then they came to a stone fence, and a little later on, an iron gate set into that fence. Cherie sat up, staring at the huge lawn that rolled away from the fence, at the magnolia trees and the weeping willows that formed little islands here and there in the wide spread of grass.

Brian stopped the car, got out, and opened the gates. Cherie sat up, staring. When he came back into the car, she asked, "Is this where you live?"

"This is River View, my home."

He drove up a winding road after closing the gate behind him, and braked to one side of a magnificent house that seemed to Cherie's eyes to go on forever. She stared up at great white columns, at windows flanked by stone carvings, at a roof ornate with moldings. Her eyes grew wider as they scanned the mansion, and she knew that she had never imagined a place so breathtaking.

He smiled down at her, lifting her bag from the car trunk. "This is where you'll live for a while. You'll like it here. At least, I hope you will."

She walked beside him as he stepped toward the house. Suddenly she felt very small and insignificant. If Brian Cutler was so wealthy, why in the world was he bothering with her? Unless, of course, he meant to seduce her in one of the bedrooms of the mansion.

Cherie scowled. After that kiss he had given her, it might be so hard to seduce her, after all. She was not quite the strong, self-sufficient girl she had always believed herself to be.

He unlocked the front door and stepped inside, putting a finger to his lips. "Be quiet, we don't want to wake my brother."

At least there was somebody else in the house. They wouldn't be all alone. Somewhat relieved, Cherie followed him on tiptoe across the big hall and up the curving staircase. The house was very still around them, and dark. Once she stumbled on the stair carpeting, and his hand came down to catch hers, to guide her up after him.

When they came to an open doorway, Brian ushered her inside, closed the door, and flicked on the light. Cherie stared at a huge mahogany tester bed, neatly made with a satin spread across it. There was a chair, a small desk, an ottoman, and off to one side, a big clothes cabinet.

Brian put down her bag and winked at her. "Get a good night's sleep. We have a lot to do tomorrow."

Cherie stood and watched as he closed the door behind him, aware that she was rather disappointed that he had not at least offered to kiss her again. Of course, she would not have let him. That was understood. But he could have tried, couldn't he?

She wandered about the room, staring at the furniture, the ceramics, the oil paintings on the wall. It came to her that Brian Cutler must be very well-to-do to be able to live in such a mansion. Hmmmm. He was quite wealthy, so why was he bothering with her? She was poor, she didn't have any more than a couple of dollars to rub together. And it didn't seem that he was about to seduce her, either, leaving her alone in this big bedroom. She glanced at the white door, saw that it was furnished with a huge lock.

She could lock him out, if he had any ideas about sneaking in on her in the middle of the night. The middle of the night? It was well past that now. Cherie yawned and decided that she might as well go to bed.

She did not dream that night, or if she did, she did not remember it. When she woke, she realized it must be rather late. Sunlight was flooding into her room and she could hear faint sounds from belowstairs.

Hurriedly she ran from the bed to the bathroom, deciding on a quick shower. Under the flooding waters, she told herself that last night Brian had said they were going to be busy today. That meant she had to wear her best clothes, she supposed, and made a face. She didn't have many good clothes.

Well, at least she had brought a cowl-collared maroon dress last summer, with front and back tucking and graceful sleeves. She would wear that, with maybe a pin to offset it, at the breast. Cherie hoped it was not too wrinkled from being in the bag.

She dressed swiftly, putting on fresh underthings and then wriggling into the Kappi creation. A quick glance in the mirror told her that the maroon color did things for her, and she spent a few minutes in arranging her long golden hair in an upsweep.

There came a knock on the door.

"Come on in," she called. "I'm decent."

Brian poked his head around the edge of the door. His eyes grew wide at sight of her. She smiled at him, liking his admiration.

"Will I do?" she asked.

"Hey, you're beautiful!"

"I wouldn't go that far."

He came into the room, walking toward her slowly. "I would. I don't think I've ever seen anyone so lovely." He hesitated, and then got that impish grin. "Except once."

"Ohhh?"

Cherie was aware of a quick stab of jealousy, and told herself not to be ridiculous. Brian Cutler meant nothing to her, he was just someone who was protecting her. Against that, of course, she did not know, except that somebody seemed to want her dead.

"Not to worry. The woman I'm talking about has been dead a long time."

She stared at him, knowing that he was piling mystery on mystery. What dead woman could he mean? No matter, if she were dead.

"You enjoy puzzling me, don't you?" she asked.

He put out his hand, caught hers. "Not really. Now, come along and have some breakfast. We have some visiting to do today."

"Visiting?"

She wasn't at all sure that she wanted to visit anyone. On the other hand, Cherie felt that she had to do something while staying here with Brian. She had never been one to sit around and twiddle her thumbs. She walked with him to the door and down the hall, and caught a whiff of fragrant coffee perking.

As they came into the dining room, she noted that silver serving dishes had been arranged on a buffet, together with a huge percolator. Brian gestured at the array.

"Help yourself. There's eggs, bacon, toast. If you'd rather have something like griddle cakes, just say the word."

"Only coffee, thanks."

He drew back to glance at her. "Better eat a good breakfast. We're taking a drive. I don't know when we can have lunch."

She paused in the act of filling a cup with coffee to eye him. "Where is it we're going?"

"Ever hear of Oak Haven?"

Cherie frowned. The words were vaguely familiar, she had heard of them recently, or read of them. She shook her head. "No, but it does sound as though I've read of it lately."

"It's a big estate on the other side of the city, along the river. Belonged to a family named Mannering."

She shook her head, then carried her cup to the table. She sipped the coffee as she watched Brian fill a platter with eggs and several strips of bacon, then place slices of toast beside them.

He sat near her, began to eat. Cherie watched him with amusement. He certainly seemed to enjoy eating. As for herself . . . She shuddered. She could never get all that food down inside her in the morning. It didn't seem right, somehow.

"You're missing a lot." Brian smiled at her as he chewed. "Have some."

"No, thanks."

"Helps keep up your energy."

"For what?"

His eyes studied her, and to Cherie they seemed to gleam with an inner amusement. "For what the day may prove to you."

Cherie felt annoyance. "Will you stop speaking in riddles! If you have something to tell me that I ought to know, come out and say it."

He grinned. "Not yet. You'll know in time."

She rose to refill her cup, then brought it back to the table. As she sat down, she asked, "Has anyone ever told you how infuriating you can be?"

"Only you. Mostly I'm quite charming, very well-behaved, I'm helpful to old ladies and I never, never kick dogs."

"Do you ever get kicked yourself? Right now I have the urge to administer a good, swift kick to your shins."

His face filled with mock surprise. "After all the trouble I'm going to, saving your life and—"

"And?"

Brian shook his head. "Can't tell you."

Cherie clenched her fists. Suddenly she swung one of those fists at him, half playfully, half in earnest. He seemed to have been waiting for some such move on her part, though. He caught her fist, brought it to his lips, and kissed it. Cherie stared at him, eyes wide.

"I'm glad you did that," he said softly. "It shows you have a temper. Good! It means that I'm right. Or, at least, it helps."

He sat back and beamed at her. He still held on to her fist, she noted. And her flesh tingled. Her eyes locked with his and she sat there with her heart starting to pound crazily.

She made herself talk. "Why? Why does my temper please you so much?"

"Not yet. You'll have to wait a little while."

"You really are very annoying, you know."

"Just trust me."

She sat back, drawing her hand from his. She lifted her cup and drank coffee, trying to tell herself that this was not a crazy dream, that Brian Cutler was a sane man—he was a lawyer, after all—and that maybe he did have her best interests at heart.

It was rather difficult to do, because all he ever seemed to do was add question upon question until she thought she would go mad. Why did anyone want her dead? He seemed to know, or guess—yet he would say nothing. Who was this dead lady who was so beautiful? What had she, Cherie Marsan, to do with a dead woman? Why was he so happy to see her temper flare up?

Ha! He hadn't seen her temper. When she was fully aroused, her temper quite honestly got the better of her. Naturally, she fought against it, she didn't want to be thought a virago. Cherie sighed. Life was very difficult, at times.

"One more cup and then we're off," he said, getting to his feet and reaching for her cup.

As he returned with two full cups, Cherie said, "This is quite a home you have. You do live here, don't you?"

"Of course. My brother Joe and I own it. He's long since gone to the office. Right now he's handling both our cases while I'm working on yours."

Cherie gulped and stared. "My what?"

"Your case."

She couldn't help it. She slapped her hands down flat on the tabletop, making the coffeecups dance. "Will you talk sense! I don't have a case! I don't need a lawyer! I'm just an unknown artist! Now, if you can't tell me what this is all about, I'm going to get up and walk out of here and you'll never see me again."

To her annoyance, he shook his head, eyeing her gently, as he might an obnoxious child. His lips curved into a gentle smile. "Easy, easy. Can't you trust me just a little longer? Give me a day or two at least."

Cherie scowled, glowering at him. "Why?"

"Because I want you to stay alive, because I want you to live a long and very enjoyable life." His hand came out to capture hers. "Please, Cherie."

She could not stay angry with him, not when he got that look on his face and his eyes seemed almost to eat her up. Besides, his hand holding hers was strong yet gentle, and she liked the feel of it, gripping her. It seemed to bring them a little closer together.

"All right," she mumbled, staring down at the table. "For a couple more days, then." She lifted her eyes and glared at him. "But no more mysteries!"

Brian seemed to consider that, head tilted to one side. "All right. If I can manage it, that is. Right now, it's safer for you to remain in the dark about what it is I'm going to do."

She thought about the gas that had been turned on in her little apartment. Maybe the guy was right, after all. Apparently, somebody did want her dead. Why, she could not imagine, though she had the sneaking feeling that Brian Cutler knew. Okay, then. She would go along with him and whatever it was he had in mind for her to do.

After all, this wasn't hard to take. Her eyes ran around the big dining room, studying the highly polished furniture, the silver serving salvers, the thick rug, the exquisite window drapes. All this spoke of wealth, and wealth was something Cherie Marsan had had nothing to do with, all her life.

She could take as much of this as Brian was willing to give her. That bed last night had been something. She had slept like a baby in it; it had seemed to cradle her, take her body into its softness and cushion her. She had waked this morning feeling very refreshed.

Brian finished the last of his coffee, put the cup down, and raised his eyebrows. "Ready?"

They walked out into the late-spring sunshine. It was a warm day, Cherie was a little sorry she had worn such a fancy dress. Brian was well-dressed, too, in slacks and a blazer. He looked like a very successful businessman, she told herself.

He opened the door of the Granada for her. She liked that thoughtfulness in him, that politeness. She had always had to do for herself. There had never been anyone to open doors for her, to pour her coffee, to care whether she was comfortable or not.

Well, there were her parents, naturally. But she had not seen them for a couple of years, ever since she had come downriver to live in New Orleans. She wondered if they ever worried about her. By rights, she ought to have gone back to little Row Landing to visit her mother and father from time to time. She had written to them often enough, but she had a guilty feeling that a letter might not have been enough.

Brian drove through the spring sunshine, taking his time, pointing out an old landmark here and there. Cherie saw houses set far back from the road, houses with a quiet dignity about them, with white colonnades and fancy rooftops. He went by way of Airline Highway until he came to Lake Pontchartrain Causeway over the lake, and then his speed increased.

They drove through countryside where Cherie had never been before, down roads lined with trees. She was lost in staring, in telling herself that all she was seeing was a part of history. Here had been great plantations in the past, where very wealthy families had lived. Most of them were gone now, but a few still remained.

At last, Brian turned in at a very fancy gateway of iron scrollwork supported by stone pillars. In the scrollwork she could make out the name—fashioned by twisted iron flowers: Oak Haven. She glanced at Brian, who nodded.

"This is where we're headed," he told her. Then added with a faint grin, "It's where that woman lived. You know, the one who was as beautiful as you."

"Am I going to see her?"

"Sure. That's the whole purpose of this trip."

She eyed him carefully, wondering if he were quite sane. Oh, he seemed sane enough, it was just those little hints and innuendos he kept tossing at her that puzzled her so much. Oh, well. Let him have his little joke, if it was a joke. She would know how to handle him when it happened. Or she thought she did, anyhow.

There were other cars grouped here and there, she saw as they pulled into a parking space. A bus or two also. She looked at him wonderingly. "Seems like half New Orleans is here."

"It's visiting day. This used to be the Mannering estate. Still is, of course. But the estate lawyers have opened it to the public for a time, until the estate of the old man is settled."

"What old man?"

"Josiah Mannering. Surely you've heard of him?"

"Who hasn't? He was one of the richest men in all the South. I've heard he was worth a billion dollars. I think he made his money in shipping."

"In shipping, in oil, in the stock market, in real estate. You name it, old Josiah had a hand in it. A big hand, too, that scooped up most of the profits—and anything he went into showed a profit, believe me. He even owned land in Europe, here and there, and I've heard also that he owned some diamond mines in South Africa. The guy was a living legend."

"Hey, now. His heirs must be dancing a jig step right about now."

Brian chuckled. "I'm sure they are. But come on. Let's go inside and take the tour."

Cherie glanced at him curiously. He seemed very excited, almost as though he expected something to happen. She shrugged and stepped out when he opened the door, walked with her to the huge front doors that were open now. A man sat behind a desk with a string of tickets to one side of him and a big metal box to the other.

Brian reached for his wallet, paid their fees. Then he caught her hand and drew her down the hall toward a magnificent oak staircase. It curved upward toward the second floor, and where it curved, the wall above it was hung with a number of oil paintings.

Cherie took a step forward, and stared, speechless.

One of those oil painting was of . . . *her!*

4

She was vaguely aware that Brian was standing close beside her, staring down at her even as her own eyes were raised to that picture on the wall above her. She felt her heart pounding. It could not be! It was as though she herself had sat for that painting.

She was clad in an old-fashioned dress—or at least, the woman in the painting was—and her blond hair made a wreath about her beautiful face. She held a fan in her hands, and there was a queenliness about her that told Cherie this woman must have been someone very important.

Cherie could not tear away her eyes. It was almost like looking into a mirror. The shape of the lips, the tilt of the nose, the intense blue of her eyes, were exactly the same as her own! If she didn't know better, she would have bet money that at some time recently, she herself had posed for that painting.

She grew aware of Brian and turned to look at him, eyes wide. "Who was she?" she asked breathlessly.

"Lavinia Mannering, Josiah Mannering's great grandmother. Beautiful woman, wasn't she?"

"Brian, it's me!" she exclaimed ungrammatically.

"You notice the resemblance, do you?"

"Resemblance? I could be her twin."

"So I think, myself. Her twin, or maybe her daughter. Or even, perhaps, a descendant."

Cherie laughed faintly. "Some descendant. If I were related to her, I'd be rich, wouldn't I?"

"Very rich, indeed."

Something about the way he spoke attracted her eyes to his face. There was a grimness to his tanned face, a hardness in his eyes, that surprised her.

"Well, I'm not rich. I'm practically penniless. So don't be tempting me by putting ideas in my head." She ran a hand over the banister of the staircase, admiring its gloss.

31

Wistfully she murmured, "I wonder what it was like, all those years ago, living in a place such as this. It must have been like heaven."

"Want to take a look around? I've been here before, I can give you a guided tour." He caught her hand, drew her from the few steps they had ascended, and brought her into a room where everything was spotless.

Cherie stared at exquisite furniture, at satin coverings, at magnificent mirrors. There were sofas here, and chairs, and off in one corner of the huge room, a grand piano. Oriental rugs and carpets were on the floor, there were exquisite paintings on the walls—Cherie recognized several original Fragonards, those two off to one side she was positive were oils done by David, and facing her was a magnificent naval scene that was surely a Turner!

Her eyes ran all over the room, and she knew deep inside her that the contents of this room alone were worth a fortune. She shook her head. It was hard to understand how so much wealth could be accumulated under one roof. Josiah Mannering had been a very wealthy man, indeed.

"It's scary, it's so lovely," she whispered.

"And expensive."

She turned to him. "Have you any idea of how wealthy the old man was?"

Brian grinned. "A billion, at least. Oh, I know there aren't very many billionaires in the world, but Josiah Mannering was one of them. His holdings are worldwide, he maintained a battery of lawyers and accountants just to let him know how rich he was and to make certain that nobody else got their hands on it."

Cherie sighed. "His children are very lucky people."

"He doesn't have any. Oh, he had a son, a long time ago, but the son died."

"Unmarried, I suppose."

"Oh, he got married, all right. He and his wife had a child, too, but nobody knows what happened to it."

Cherie gasped. "Nobody knows! But that can't be. Wouldn't the old man make certain about that? I mean, after all . . ."

Her words died off. She felt sorrow touch her for a moment. Imagine that little baby growing up and being heir to such a fortune yet never learning about it. It was so sad. The little child might be desperately in need of money, too. Little child? Well, not anymore, she guessed. He or she must be about twenty or so. Her own age, even.

Brian was saying, "Old Josiah made a search, naturally. He was in Europe at the time his daughter-in-law and his grandchild disappeared. Nobody knows where they went or why. The earth seems to have opened up and swallowed them."

Cherie sighed. "A shame. A tragic shame."

Brian smiled down at her. "Hey, cheer up. All that was long ago. Twenty years or more. Let's go look at the rest of the house."

She brightened, seeing his smile. "Sure, Brian. Now that we're here, we might as well enjoy this. Though I do feel sorry for that child. Was it a boy or a girl?"

"A girl. Her name was Clarissa."

"Clarissa Mannering. It has a nice ring to it."

He put his arm about her shoulders, guiding her out into the hallway and to another room. Cherie found her eyes caught and held by the handsome furniture, the paintings on the walls, the rich rugs, and very beautiful decorations. They moved from room to room; they inspected the huge dining room, the vast kitchen, the downstairs den, and the music room.

It took them close to four hours to go through the mansion. Brian seemed to be in no hurry; indeed, to Cherie he appeared to want to linger here and there, pointing out the marvelous pieces of furniture collected from all over the world by old Josiah Mannering, the fabulous rugs, the extraordinary art collection that graced the walls of the great house.

It was almost as though Brian were showing the place to a prospective buyer, Cherie thought from time to time. She paid attention to him, she listened as he talked, she was grateful for his concern and interest. Yet it seemed to her that he had some ulterior purpose in mind, a purpose she could not understand.

When they finally came out into the open air and turned to give the mansion one last look, Brian said, "A tremendous inheritance, this. And the house and grounds are only a small part of the estate."

"What do you mean?" Cherie wondered.

"Old Josiah Mannering had most of his money tied up in business ventures. In oil, in shipping, in stocks and

bonds. Whoever inherits all this will be one of the richest
people in the world."

"I suppose so." She sighed. "I just can't imagine all this
wealth."

"Well, let's say this was all yours. What would you do
with it?"

She stared at him. "Have you committed to the nut
house. That's where you belong, thinking such thoughts."

He laughed and caught her arm, drawing her toward his
Granada. "Maybe I am crazy, after all. But I am interested in you, I want to learn all about you."

Cherie felt a sudden tenderness. It was nice of Brian to
take this interest in her, to want her safe and secure. She
owed him a lot. She leaned against him as they neared the
Granada, and smiled up at him.

"Well, first of all, I'm an artist."

"Oh, before that. Long ago, when you were a child.
What's the first thing you remember?"

Cherie laughed, then sobered. "A big doll. Only it
wasn't a doll, not exactly. I think now it was a big stuffed
toy of some sort. I used to sleep with my arms about it."

She paused and frowned. "Strange. All I remember is
that stuffed toy and a woman." She shook her head. "It
wasn't Mother Marsan, it was somebody else. I think it
was my real mother, though I can't be sure. The Marsans
adopted me, you know."

"I didn't, but that makes no difference. Go on."

He opened the car door and she slid in on the seat. The
memories were coming back now, as Brian went around to
get in behind the wheel. Little bits and glimpses of her
early life, of the house where she lived with the Marsans,
of her school days, of her first interest in drawing and
painting.

When he started the engine, she said, "I can remember
crying one night. I think something bad had happened and
I was frightened. But I was in my mother's arms and she
was walking with me. Oh, a long way. She was hurt, I
seem to remember, because she was crying too, even as
she was begging me not to."

Cherie shook her head. "I haven't thought about that in
years. When I was little, that scene was like a recurring
nightmare to me. As I grew older, it sort of faded away."

They were silent for a time, and Cherie wondered why

Brian was asking all these things about her early life. He was probably just making conversation, she decided.

Then he asked, "What else do you remember about your mother?"

"Not very much. Just that tiny bit. After that, all I can recall has to do with the Marsans. They're wonderful people, they're descended from the French who came into Louisiana from Acadia. You know that old poem by Longfellow? *Evangeline*? Well, the Marsans' ancestors came from Acadia, just as did Gabriel and Evangeline herself.

"Only they were luckier than those two. They traveled in the same boat, the Marsans and the Senacs; they were friends, back in Acadia. Mother Marsan is descended from the Senacs." Cherie sighed. "Every time I read *Evangeline*, I would cry toward the end, when Evangeline finally found her Gabriel as an old man on his deathbed."

His hand was holding hers, she noted, as they drove along, and for some reason, Cherie was grateful. She was feeling sad as she always did at the thought of Evangeline, and his touch seemed somehow reassuring.

They were moving past some very high grass, along a lonely country road. To the left was a field of big rocks, tumbled about and scattered here and there. Suddenly Brian's hand was gone from hers; it was on the wheel and he was swinging that wheel almost wildly.

Out of the corner of her eye, Cherie saw a big black car shoot out from a dirt side road. It was almost on top of them and it was traveling at high speed.

"Damn!" yelled Brian even as he fought the car in its wild careening.

There was a faint scrape of fender on fender, a scream of grating metal.

The Granada was on two wheels, veering toward those huge rocks. In a moment it was going to crash into them. The car would crumple—the car would burst into flames—they were going to be killed!

Cherie could not breathe. She opened her mouth, her eyes were wide, she clenched her teeth. In a moment now, she would be dead!

Then . . .

Somehow Brian got control of the Ford. It swerved, just missing the rocks, and came back down onto the road. The big black car was hurtling past, and Cherie caught a glimpse of two bulky men in that car, peering out as their car rocked and slid past them.

Brian braked the Granada, brought it to a stop.

The black car faded off into the distance.

Cherie gasped for air, turning her white face toward Brian. His own face was pale, strained, and there was agony in his eyes as he looked at her.

"They tried to kill us," he was saying.

She could not speak, she was too frozen. A moment ago, they had almost piled into those big rocks. She realized she was shaking. All she could do was stare at Brian Cutler.

He put out his arms, caught her, brought her in against his chest, holding her. Her heart was banging away wildly, she hardly realized even yet that they had escaped serious injury, perhaps death.

"That was deliberate," Brian was murmuring. "Those men wanted to kill us."

Cherie found her voice. "Oh, Brian. It was an accident. No more than that. If it hadn't been for you . . ."

She shivered. If Brian had not been at the wheel, if he had not reacted so swiftly, their mangled bodies would be lying in a heap of twisted, burning metal right now. His arms squeezed her, held her firmly.

"You all right?" he asked after a time.

She tried to smile. "I-I think so. It all happened so suddenly."

His face grew hard. "They were waiting there for us, ready to come slamming out at us."

She drew back to look up into his hard face. "You—you make it sound deliberate."

"It *was* deliberate. Those men tried to kill us. Especially you."

"But . . ."

She remembered the gas heater that had been turned on while she had been asleep, and her gasp was loud. Could it be? Could someone—she had no idea who it might be—want her dead badly enough to go to all these lengths? It just didn't seem believable.

"Why?" she wailed. "Why would anyone want to kill me?"

Brian was silent for such a long time that she scowled at him. A suspicion crept into her head. Did he know the answer to that? Could he possibly understand what motive those men would have to want her dead?

"Do you?" she wondered. "Do you know the answer to that?"

"Wait," he told her gently. "Just wait a little while."

"Wait?" she howled. "Wait for what? Until I'm dead?"

He sought to soothe her. "I'm here. I'll take care of you. You're still alive, and I mean to keep you that way, believe me."

She began to beat upon his shoulders with her fists. Fear was inside her, but more than the fear was the uncertainty of why anyone would desire her to die. If only she could know the reason! She had never harmed anyone. Always, she had been friendly and understanding to anyone with whom she had come in contact.

As she babbled this out and went on pounding his shoulders, Brian caught her hands and held them. Tears were running down her cheeks, she stared at him through a misty blur.

"You're the only one I have to t-turn to," she pleaded. "You're the only person who seems to know anything. What is it? Why should my death benefit anyone? What reason is there to kill me?"

Brian kissed her hands, still holding them. He was very gentle with her, Cherie realized. He was ignoring her hysteria, he was doing what he could to calm her.

"We're going to the Marsans," he said softly. "Right now. I was going to wait until tomorrow, but you're too upset to wait."

"What are they going to tell you?" she half-sobbed.

"Something that will make a big difference in your life." He hesitated, then muttered almost to himself, "If I wasn't quite positive before, I am now. So sit back like a good girl and just leave everything to me."

Cherie glared at him through her tears. "You always make everything so mysterious. What's the big deal? If you know why those men tried to kill me, why won't you tell me?"

"Because you wouldn't believe me."

She sat back against the seat, pulling her hands from his. Anger was alive in her, she wanted to strike out at Brian for being so closemouthed, but beneath the anger was a real fear. Alive, she was dangerous to someone.

That much was fairly obvious. Ah, but to whom? To whom? And why wouldn't Brian tell her?

Ha! Because she wouldn't believe him, he had said. She would believe any crazy reason he told her. She would, she would! It was the uncertainty of not knowing that ate into her.

Brian started the car and drove on. He drove carefully, she noted; his eyes were always moving as though he suspected that black car to come slamming out at him once again, at some country crossroads. Yet they moved forward, away from Lake Pontchartrain and toward Baton Rouge.

After they had ridden for more than an hour, Brian glanced at her. "You getting hungry?"

Cherie shook her head. Food was furthest away from her thoughts. Yet she asked, "How about you? I couldn't eat a thing, but I suppose you're half starved, even if you did eat a big breakfast."

He laughed. "I manage to do away with three meals a day. Keeps me healthy."

Cherie sniffed. Men and their appetites! They couldn't be content with a cup or two of coffee in the morning and then a meal at night. They had to be eating, eating, always eating. Her eyes slid toward Brian. Hmmm. He didn't look as though food did him any harm, though. He seemed slim enough, though solidly made. And he had great wide shoulders.

"Stop anywhere you like," she said. "I don't want you to starve to death."

Brian laughed. "Since we're going to be together for quite some time, I guess it's a good idea for you to get used to my habits, at that."

"Oh? What habits are those?"

"Nothing special. Just eating and sleeping. The usual things a person does to stay alive. Ooops. Sorry. Didn't mean to bring up the subject of staying alive."

"It's okay," she whispered. "I'm over my fright. Or I think I am."

He reached out for her hand, and Cherie resisted the impulse to draw it away. So let him hold it. What difference did it make? Besides, it added to her feeling that they were in this thing together. They might as well be friends.

The Ford drove on through the early afternoon.

They stopped at a sandwich shop outside Baton Rouge.

Cherie was not hungry, but as soon as she stepped inside the shadowed room and caught the smells of baking bread and frying meats, she decided that she might as well have a sandwich and a cup of coffee. No sense in sitting there while Brian ate, watching him devour each mouthful, and merely twiddle her thumbs, waiting for him.

She ordered a ham sandwich and he decided on a roast beef on rye.

"What are you going to ask the Marsans?" she asked as the waitress brought them coffee.

He smiled at her. "To tell me what you were like as a litle girl. Things they remember about you. When you first started painting."

"I could tell you all that."

"But not the way they could. You see yourself only with your own eyes. I want an objective view."

Cherie sighed. "But why?"

"Things I'd like to know." He moved the knife and fork beside his plate. "I've done some research on this matter and—"

"On what matter?" she interrupted.

He hesitated. "On you, I guess I could say. Or at least, on your connections."

"There you go again, making with the mystery. What do you mean, my connections?"

His hand caught hers, squeezed it. His eyes were very intent, almost burning as they stared back at her. "Will you get the chip off your shoulder? Everything I'm doing or am about to do—or have done lately, for that matter—has been done with only your good in mind. You keep questioning me as though I were some sort of enemy. I'm not, believe me."

The waitress was there with the sandwiches, and Cherie began to eat. The ham sandwich was delicious, she had to admit, and was surprised. She usually ate a sandwich when she was at the cathedral railing displaying her artwork, but then she was working and needed her energy. All she was doing now was riding around Louisiana with Brian Cutler. That didn't take very much out of her.

Still, she might as well keep her strength up.

When they were finished eating, they had second cups of coffee. Brian said, "I'm going to ask a favor of you. Don't interfere with me when I speak with the Marsans, okay?"

She eyed him suspiciously. "Why not?"

"I don't want you frightening them."

Cherie gaped at him. "*Frightening* them? I'd never do anything like that! I love them both."

"Sure you do. But, believe me, when I say what I'm going to, they may be frightened."

She shook her head. "I don't understand this, not at all. And I'm not certain whether or not I like it."

"Never mind that. Will you promise?"

She considered him, studying his rather handsome face, its strong lines, the intent eyes and firm lips. Something inside her told her that she could trust this man. He might make with the mystery, but she felt that maybe he did have a very good reason for it.

Of course, she knew little or nothing about him except that he seemed to come from a good family, he appeared to have money, and he was a lawyer. A lawyer who was interested in her "case." What he had meant by that remark, she did not know, but she knew instinctively he had her good at heart.

"I promise. I'll follow your lead. I'll be quiet."

"Good girl. Remember, I'm doing all this for your good, not for any other reason."

He stood up then, and they went out to the car after he had paid the bill. Cherie saw him pause at the Granada and look around, up and down the road. Was he searching for that big black car? He opened the door and she got in.

They drove on toward Row Landing.

Cherie wondered what it was he hoped to learn from the Marsans.

5

The Marsans lived in a little cottage surrounded by a white picket fence. The lawn was large and well-tended, and here and there were bushes. Out back were small buildings, one of which was a worship where Pierre Marsan made cabinets and bookcases, chairs and tables. There was a garage for their small car, and a larger building where he stored those odds and ends of furniture he made when trade was slack, where he kept articles made on order until pickup or delivery.

Their cottage was in a lonely spot. The road that lay in front of their home was seldom used, it ran back into the woods and disappeared. Long ago there had been a lumbering outfit back in those woods, but few people alive today were old enough to remember it.

Brian pulled the Granada up before the fence, along a verge of neatly cut grass. He paused a moment, studying the house, before he shut off the motor and pocketed the key.

Cherie stared at the house, remembering it as it had been in her early childhood when it had appeared very much as it was now, except that she noted that Father Marsan had added a new coat of paint to everything fairly recently. She could remember the sound of his saw and hammer as he made a desk or perhaps a bureau in those long-ago days when she had been a child. She recalled, too, how very strange it had seemed to her to have a father who worked at home. Unlike all the other children who had attended school with her, she was the only one who could make such a claim. All the other fathers had gone off to work.

She smiled as she got out of the car. Quite often, after school, Father Marsan had let her come into his workshop to help him. He had permitted her to polish the wood on a finished piece, teaching her gently, carefully, what it was

41

she had to do, guiding her hands at first, never critical but always admiring. Under his tutelage she become quite accomplished as a furniture polisher.

She saw movement at one of the downstairs curtains. In a few moments, as she went up the walk with Brian, she saw the front door being flung open and Mother Marsan standing there, a tremulous smile on her lips, her arms flung wide.

"Cherie! I don't believe it! How are you?"

The years rushed away; it seemed to Cherie that she was a child again, being welcomed home by her mother. Tears sprang into her eyes, she gave a little cry and ran forward to be caught and held in those arms. Those arms hugged her, seemed reluctant to let her go.

Marie Marsan fought against the tears that threatened to run down her cheeks. She was small, rounded, her face seemed unlined, and her hair was dark black. Her hands caught Cherie, held her back a little as she stared at her.

"You are not the little girl who went to New Orleans to study art," she whispered. "You are a woman now."

Her eyes went past Cherie to take in Brian Cutler where he stood on the steps, smiling at her. "And who is this? Your husband? Eh? Have you gone and married, Cherie?"

Cherie smiled. "No, Mama. He's just a good friend."

"Then come in, sir. Please! Our home is your home."

"You are too kind." Brian smiled, taking the hand that was thrust out to him.

"Come in, come in, don't stand there, the two of you." Marie Marsan stepped aside, gesturing with her hand, smiling at them invitingly. "I'll go call Father. He's out back as usual, working."

"I'll go get him, Mama. I want to surprise him."

She moved past her mother, running down the hall to the back door and out across the yard on the little walk that Pierre Marsan had put in long ago. Her eyes caught sight of the crepe myrtles with their pink blossoms, the rose bushes in their neat patch of ground off to one side—these were Mama's favorites, she tended them herself with loving care—and beyond the magnolias and the oaks stood the garden with its potatoes, peas, beans, and squash. That was Papa's domain, the garden where he fussed on summer evenings after his work was done.

The door of his workshop was open to catch the breezes. Cherie went to stand in that doorway, staring as she had done so many years before, hesitating to intrude upon his labors. He was bent above a worktable, using a cloth to polish a bit of decorative carving that would be added soon enough to something he had already built.

She ran to him, caught the cloth from his fingers, and began polishing as he had taught her to do long ago. She grew aware of his quick stab of breath, of his eyes upon her.

"Cherie," he whispered, and she turned to him, half-laughing, half-crying, dropping the polishing cloth to catch him in her arms.

He kissed her cheeks, then growled. "You have been a bad girl, staying away so long. Your mother and I have missed you."

"I know, Papa. I know. But it has not been easy, selling my paintings. There are a lot of artists in New Orleans."

His eyes scanned her face. "It is not easy, eh? Well, you can come home, you know. Your room is just as you left it."

She smiled at him through her tears. "No, no. It isn't anything like that. I'm doing all right. But some men have tried to kill me and the man I am with has decided that we ought to come and see you and Mama, to try and find out why."

His strong hands caught hold of her shoulders as his eyes blazed at her. "What's this? Tried to kill you? In God's name, why? What have you done?"

"Nothing, nothing. I'm sure it's all some great big mistake. But this friend of mine—Brian Cutler is his name—is a lawyer, and he seems to think that there is some sort of reason why someone wants to get rid of me."

His face was white as he went on staring. Then he said softly, "Your mother. Have you told her anything of this?"

"Of course not! I only told you so that you would know why Brian is going to ask all sorts of questions about me."

His sharp eyes studied her. He sighed. "It has come out of the past, this danger. I felt it might, someday." He shook his head. "It will be hard, fooling your mother. She will know something's amiss."

Her arm caught him, turned him. "Come on, leave off work. Mama and Brian are in the house, talking. They will want to talk to you, too." She hugged him. "It is good to be back, to see you and Mama again. I've been away too long."

They went along the walk and into the house. Cherie could hear Brian talking, speaking of New Orleans. His voice was friendly, persuasive. It was a good voice, Cherie thought, she could imagine him using it to sway juries when he was trying a case.

As they came into the front room, Brian was standing near the fireplace, smiling. Her mother was seated, staring up at him. As they entered, she turned and smiled at Cherie, and she knew instinctively that her mother liked Brian.

He came forward now to shake her father's hand as Cherie introduced them. "I'm glad to be able to bring Cherie back to you for a visit," he said. "But there's a little more to it than that."

Pierre Marsan smiled. "And what would that little more be?"

Brian moved away, taking a few steps, frowning. He swung back, spread his hands. "There have been two attempts made on Cherie's life."

Her mother cried out, her father gasped.

Brian held up a hand. "She's safe enough, as you can see. But she needs your help. So do I, frankly." His smile was friendly, assuring. "I want to ask if either of you know why anyone would want to kill her."

Marie Marsan exclaimed. "Certainly not! She's always been a good girl, popular in school and out of it. She's always made friends easily. She had no enemies."

Her husband added heavily, "What you tell us is shocking, frightening." He moved toward Cherie, put his arms about her. "Come, Cherie, sit down. We can solve this problem, I'm sure."

He glanced at Brian, nodding his head. "Your friend there wants to help you, we know that. He is a good man, I can tell." He smiled faintly. "I have had a lot to do with men during my lifetime. I have become a good judge of them. Trust that one."

"He keeps making mysteries," Cherie muttered, glancing at Brian.

"Only for your own good, I am certain," her father said. Then he looked at Brian. "That is so, young man, isn't it?"

"It most certainly is. We all want only the best for Cherie. That's understood. All I'm asking you people is, please help me get the best for her."

Marie Marsan looked bewildered. "But what have we to do with it? We certainly want only the best for her. Always, we have acted with that in mind, ever since she . . . came to us."

Brian smiled. "Exactly. Ever since she came to you." In a quiet voice he asked, "Just how was it that she came to you?"

There was a little silence. Marie Marsan fumbled for a handkerchief, put it to her eyes. She wept a moment, then straightened and looked at her husband. "You tell him, Pierre. I-I am not up to it."

Pierre Marsan cleared his throat. "It was a long time ago, almost twenty years." He stared down at his hands. "There was a terrible storm, perhaps it was a hurricane, I do not know. But the rain was terrible, it drummed down on our roof as though each raindrop were a hailstone. Mama was saying the rosary. I can still hear her as she said her prayers while we were together in bed, listening.

"I was afraid the house might be blown away, the wind was so great. It was very dark outside. Very dark. That darkness was lighted up occasionally by vivid flashes of lightning." He smiled wryly. "I was doing some praying, too, I admit. I was afraid the lightning would strike the house, cause a fire, and burn it down."

He sighed, lifting his head. "I do not remember a more terrible storm than that one. Never! I have not been frightened many times in my life, but I was frightened that night.

"Sometime toward morning, the rain and the lightning let up a little. It was still raining, of course—it rained for two or three days solid at that time. But there was a bit of a break. The noise of the storm was not so terrible, you understand.

"It seemed to me that during that lull I heard a sound. A very faint sound, as though someone might be knocking at our front door. I decided it was merely the branch of a tree, perhaps broken off from its limb and swaying in the wind. I did not get up to investigate, may the good God forgive me.

"Not until it was light did we get out of bed. We glanced out the window, seeing trees and branches down, seeing a small lake formed overnight in the hollow off to the right. You remember that, Mama?"

Marie Marsan nodded. "It was terrifying, that storm,"

she whispered. "I prayed the whole night through." She lifted her head, looking at Cherie. "God heard my prayers, I know. He sent us Cherie."

Pierre Marsan nodded. "Yes. She was our little child of storm. Because when I opened our front door, she was there . . . with her real mother."

Cherie had sat transfixed at this recital. Her eyes touched her father, her mother, wonderingly. She could see their deep emotion, their grief and, yes, their inner delight.

Brian was leaning forward in the chair where he sat. "You are sure it was her real mother? Not a servant? Not a woman who might have found her in the storm?"

Pierre Marsan nodded heavily. "Oh, yes. We are sure. I will tell you why. Naturally, when I opened the door and saw the woman and the child, I called out to Marie, who came running. We carried them into the bedroom; I left them with my wife, to undress them both and put warm clothing about them. And the woman spoke of Cherie as her child."

"They were drenched, sodden with rain," the older woman murmured. "They were wet to their skins, though, I must admit, the baby was not quite as wet as the mother. She had sheltered her child inside a blanket and against her own body. But at what a cost!"

Pierre Marsan nodded. "The mother was ill. Whether she had been ill before being caught in the storm, I do not know. But she just lay in bed, saying nothing, barely breathing. Of course, we sent for a doctor as soon as we could. Old Doctor Fouquet came, when he could. He gave us medicine to give her, but I do not think he believed it would do any good. He kept shaking his head as he wrote out the prescription, I recall."

He sighed. "The child, of course, was perfectly healthy. She was a beautiful baby, about a year old, possibly a little more. She stayed with Marie while the doctor treated her mother, and she soon won her heart. She was happy, always laughing, she was a gift from God, as I have said."

Pierre Marsan took out a handkerchief and blew his nose. "The mother came to, for a little while, late that night. She begged us to look out for her child, she said someone would come for the baby in a day or two. And then she died."

The room was silent. Cherie was sitting with her hands

clasped together so tightly they hurt. All this that she was hearing was new to her. Never before had her parents— how else could she think of them? she asked herself—spoken or even hinted at all this.

"You see?" asked Marie Marsan. "There is nothing there to indicate that anyone would want Cherie dead."

"Of course not," Brian said softly.

Pierre Marsan nodded gloomily. "Naturally, we buried the poor woman. We did not know who she was, there was no identification on her. Nothing like a driver's license, not even a scrap of paper with an address. Nothing—except money."

"Money?" Brian asked, surprised.

"Never saw so much in my life. She had a change purse in her pocket stuffed full of bills. When I took it out and counted it, there was close to a thousand dollars in that thing." He shook his head. "More money than I ever saw at one time in my whole life, up to then.

"Now, that money didn't belong to us, to Marie and me, I mean. It was the child's. Yes, yours, Cherie. I put it in the bank in your name in dribs and drabs so that nobody would ask too many questions. I kept it in an old tin box buried in the back yard until I'd deposited the whole thing.

"Of course, that was later, after we'd tried to find out who Cherie was." He hesitated, then shrugged. "I guess we didn't try very hard. Marie and I were glad to have Cherie with us. She brightened up our lives, she made the hard work seem easy because now we were doing it for her, for her inheritance from us.

"Naturally, that was a bit later. Because after we buried that poor lady, we had to make some attempt to find out who she was, to whom the baby belonged. We read the newspapers, we even put an ad in the local paper, but nobody ever paid any mind to it. We were pretty well isolated in those days, this house of ours is in sort of a backwater place, away from your usual roads. Marie and I, we like it that way, no neighbors to pester us. Anybody who wants some furniture made knows where I live. Besides, I supply stuff to some merchants in town and in East Baton Rouge.

"I don't make a lot of money, but Marie and I don't have many needs, we grow a lot of our own food, we've owned this land free and clear for donkey's years, we

don't need many new clothes. Lately I've been able to
bank a good bit of money, because the orders keep coming in for new pieces of furniture. I cut my own wood in
the forest, I got a pickup truck to transport it.

"Back then, when Cherie came to us, we didn't have so
much, but we had food on the table and we could afford
to buy clothes for her. So as time went by and nobody
came forward to claim her, we sort of adopted her
ourselves."

He threw a shamefaced glance at her. "Maybe we did
wrong, but we loved that little girl and—"

Cherie ran to him, hugged him. Tears starting up in her
eyes, she said, "You're my father, Marie's my mother. I
have no other parents. You're both all I want."

She turned to Marie Marsan, sat down beside her on the
edge of the chair with an arm about her. Then she looked
at Brian.

"What's the need for all this? All you're doing is raking
up old memories that hurt."

"I'm trying to find a reason why someone would want
you dead, and I think I know the reason."

They all sat up suddenly and stared at him.

"What is that reason?" Pierre Marsan demanded.

"Obviously, because she's who she is. Not your daughter—somebody else's, and someone doesn't want her
found."

Cherie stared at him, scowling. "Why not? Why doesn't
anybody want me found? It doesn't make any sense at
all."

"Oh, yes, it does, my dear," said Pierre Marsan. "I have
the feeling that you may be the heiress to something pretty
important." His eyes looked hard at Brian Cutler. "Is that
correct, sir?"

"Right on the nose."

Cherie gaped at him. For a moment excitement ran
through her, then she realized that Brian must only be
clutching at straws. "That's ridiculous. How could I be a
danger to anyone?"

Brian grinned at her. "Just by being alive."

She turned to her mother. "Did you ever know such an
infuriating man, Mama? Sometimes I could just go over
and scratch him!"

Marie Marsan smiled faintly. "I've often had the same
feeling about your papa, dear. There are times when I

could give him a good shaking. But I find that he had his reasons for his actions or his nonactions, and that they're usually pretty good ones. It seems to me that this young man has his own reasons for being so mysterious.

"If I had to guess, I'd say that his main reason is your continued safety."

Brian stood up and gave a mock bow. "Congratulations, Mrs. Marsan. I only wish your adopted daughter had your intelligence."

"Oh, is that so?" demanded Cherie, clenching her fists.

He spread his hands. "If I told you what I had in mind, you'd hoot and laugh at me. You might not even listen."

Pierre Marsan was looking from Brian to Cherie. He said then, very softly, "I get the feeling that this is a very serious matter, Cherie. That your young man is always thinking what is best for you. Meaning your safety, first of all, and then whatever it is he has in mind about your true identity."

Brian nodded. "Exactly, sir. I want to help her, and there are times when I wonder if that's what she wants me to do."

Cherie scowled and studied the toe of her shoe. Deep inside her, she realized that Brian was helping her. All along, ever since that night he had saved her from being asphyxiated by gas, everything he had done had been done only with her good in mind. Maybe even before that, when he had asked her to paint him a self-portrait, for that matter. She slid a glance at him under her long yellow lashes.

He was looking at her, and she was struck by the tenderness in his eyes. She was acting like a spoiled child, she had been acting that way all along.

"It's what I want you to do," she said slowly, her words muffled slightly. Then more loudly, she snapped, "But I want to know what's going on, and you won't tell me."

"I will, when I feel it's the right time."

Their eyes were still locked. A flush came up from her throat into her face at the way he was staring at her. There was a gentle tenderness deep in those black eyes of his, and Cherie felt something inside her respond to it.

Her father muttered, "Sometimes it is not good to know everything, Cherie. Sometimes it is better to remain in the dark."

Her mother was patting her hand, as she had been wont to do years ago when she had been small, when something or other had bothered her.

"You're all against me," Cherie said then, but lightly, with a little laugh. "All right, have your mystery. Just tell me what you want me to do and I'll do it. No more questions. I promise."

Brian grinned at her, nodding. "That's what I want to hear. I'm your lawyer, I'm acting in your best interests, believe me. Someday you'll thank me."

Ha! He was acting as though he had the key to a magic box in his pocket, a box that, when opened, would hold all sorts of good things for her. Well, she had lost her belief in such make-believe boxes long ago. There were no such things.

Her mother stood. "Come, Cherie. We will go into the kitchen and prepare some cake and coffee. After that, you will stay for dinner, both of you."

"I'm afraid we can't stay for dinner, Mrs. Marsan," Brian said. "We have a long drive back to New Orleans. However, cake and coffee sounds very good."

Marie Marsan sighed. "It is always like this. Cherie never comes to visit us, and when she comes, it is always that she must run. Oh, well."

"I'll come back to stay for a few days, Mama," Cherie promised as she followed the older woman into the kitchen. "After this is all over."

When they were alone, the older woman turned to her, clasping her hands and holding them. "You take good care of yourself, Cherie. You and your father are all I have in the world. Just this place, and you. If anything happened to you . . ."

The woman swallowed hard.

Cherie put her arms about her and hugged her. "Don't you worry, Mama. Brian won't let anything happen to me. He watches over me as though I were a gold mine that was all his."

Marie Marsan laughed, her pretty eyes flashing. "I think you are more to him than any gold mine. I have seen the way he looks at you."

"Ha! You're just imagining things, Mama."

Ah, but was she? Cherie wondered at that, and wondered even more at why her heart was racing so swiftly all of a sudden. Brian Cutler meant nothing to her, as she meant nothing to him. He was just a lawyer helping a client.

Wasn't he?

6

They drove toward New Orleans in the early dusk, sitting side by side, with a contentment in them both. It had been very pleasant back there with the Marsans, the cake and coffee had been excellent, and sitting at the dining-room table, Cherie had basked in the talk and laughter. It was too bad it had to end so soon.

Brian had been most agreeable; it was almost as though he had learned what it was he had driven here to learn, and was appreciative of it. He and Pierre had gotten along so smoothly and easily, in such a friendly manner, that Cherie was vaguely surprised. They seemed to like each other, despite their different backgrounds, and when they had parted, Brian had shaken the older man's hand and promised to return as soon as possible and to bring Cherie with him.

She glanced at him now, asking herself what it was that he would not tell her. She knew now, of course, that the Marsans were not her real parents. They had taken her in as a child, they loved her, but . . .

"You must have some idea," she found herself saying, "who my real parents are." She sat up straighter. "That was the whole idea, wasn't it, in taking me back to the Marsans. To make sure they weren't my father and mother."

"I had to find out."

Cherie scowled. "But why?"

His grin was sudden. "Because I have a good idea as to who you really are." Excitement crept into his voice. "And, wow! What a news story this will be."

"What do you mean, news story?"

Brian hesitated, then shook his head. "Maybe I spoke out of turn just now. It's something I'd rather keep to myself for a little while longer. I'll tell you tomorrow, okay?"

Cherie gritted her teeth. This man was the most exas-

52

perating person she had ever met. Always, he surrounded himself with mystery. Well, not himself, exactly. But her. Yes, it was she about whom he put this pall of mystery. Who was she that, when word about her got out, it would mean so much excitement?

"Sometimes I think I almost hate you," she muttered. "Must you be so superior?"

He braked the car and turned to her. They were on a lonely stretch of road, there were no cars in sight. At least he was being careful, she told herself. His hands reached out and caught hers. He tugged at her, brought her closer to him.

"Believe me, please," he whispered. "I have only your welfare in mind, I'm only considering your future happiness."

"You have a funny way of showing it!"

His hand was sliding up behind her neck, under her spill of hair. Almost it seemed that his hand was drawing her toward him, because she was moving closer, until her mouth was inches from his own. His eyes burned down into hers and Cherie felt herself getting weak.

The car was oddly silent. Indeed, all outdoors beyond the car was very quiet, too. In that cessation of sound, he leaned closer and then his lips were on hers, kissing her. Cherie would not be a woman if she did not sense the hunger in that kiss, the tenderness and love. She responded to it, forgetting all about common sense; her arms came up to go about him and she hugged him just as fiercely as he was holding her.

In time, he let her go and she sank back into her seat, staring at him. She had sensed the passion in him held in leash, she understood that he wanted her as a man wants a woman.

He was fighting with some inner urge, she knew. Then he said, "I shouldn't have done that. I'm not sorry, but I shouldn't have."

"Why not?"

Brian hesitated. "You're my client."

"Client?" she asked, surprised.

He glanced at her. "If I'm to be your lawyer, then you're my client. And lawyers don't go around kissing their clients."

"I should hope not!"

He grinned. "I never have before, you know. But there's something about you . . ."

Cherie fought down her anger. After being kissed like that, to be told that he regarded her only as a client! Ha! It was enough to get any girl's blood in a boil. He couldn't even be honest with himself.

She squirmed closer so that their bodies were in contact. She knew he was uncomfortable, being so close to her, that her nearness was doing things to him. Good! Served him right.

"You like me, don't you?" She smiled up at him flirtatiously.

"Of course I like you. You're beautiful, you're pleasant, you're fun to be with. But I am your lawyer."

"I don't need a lawyer."

"Oh, yes, you do. Very much."

"I'm not suing anybody."

"Not exactly. But . . ."

He was shaking his head, obviously ill-at-ease. Cherie grinned at him, delighting in this effect she was having on him. She had never before felt this way about any man. If only he wouldn't act so—so lawyerish! If only he would stop talking and take her in his arms again and kiss her. That was what he ought to be doing!

"But what?" she asked sweetly.

"I can't tell you. Not yet. Tomorrow."

"You realize," she went on just as sweetly, "that you are the craziest man I've never known? You are an unadulterated nut of the first water. Personally, I think you're mad."

"I am." He nodded. "I am all those things. But I have only your best interests at heart."

"What do you know about my best interests?"

"Someday you'll thank me for all this," he muttered gloomily. "I just hope you'll forgive me for having grabbed you and kissed you a few times. Twice, as a matter of fact."

And why only twice, Brian Cutler? I know you want to hold me in your arms and cover me with kisses. So why don't you?

"That's not my fault," she said out loud.

"I'd better start the car."

Sure! Run away from me. Keep busy with the car so

you don't have to fight the temptation of taking me in your arms and kissing me again. Coward!

She pulled away, to sit beside him glowering into the early darkness as he started up the engine and drove on along the road. What was the matter with the guy? He was a red-blooded man, wasn't he? By rights, he ought to have parked somewhere with her and just grabbed her and made love to her.

We-ell, maybe not made love, exactly. That might be going a little too far. But he could have kissed her and hugged her and told her that he loved her, couldn't he? Of course he could. He was a coward, a sissy, a nincompoop. Cherie gritted her teeth.

Hmmm. She wondered if they would be alone in that big house tonight. Brian had said his brother lived there, too, but she hadn't seen him. If they had the house to themselves, maybe he would get up enough courage to hug and kiss her there. Cherie sat back and dreamed, thinking about that.

As the car moved along, she found her thoughts sliding toward tomorrow. He was going to tell her tomorrow why all the mystery about her, and about who she was. Cherie sniffed. Well, who was she? Not a Marsan, that was plain enough.

Ah! Was it that she was a—bastard?

No! She would not believe that. Brian was making too much of his little mystery for that. He had something to tell her about herself, she understood that. It couldn't be that she was an illegitimate child. That would make no sense at all.

Who was she, then? What was so important about her that—that those men would want her dead? Fear crept into Cherie at that thought, and she slid somewhat nervously closer to Brian. Nobody would want her dead if she were a nobody, would they? But she was just an artist, no one of any importance.

She shook her head. It made no sense, none at all.

"Tired?" he asked after a time.

"No. I'm just sitting here thinking."

"About what?"

"Oh, about a lot of things. Who I am, for one. About those men who want me dead. Why should anyone want me dead? I'm no danger to anybody."

"Oh, yes, you are, Cherie."

He would not elaborate on that, though she teased and taunted him for the rest of the ride. "Just be patient," he would say (which added to her impatience). "Until tomorrow. Only a few hours away. Can't you wait that long?"

It was not that she could not be patient. It was the idea that he knew something important about her and would not say what it was. After all, if it was about her, shouldn't she be the one to be told? It irritated her and she let him know it.

The great mansion known as River View was lighted up as Brian pulled along the drive. Just ahead of them was a car—a sleek Continental—that was just coming to a halt. Cherie wondered who it might be. Probably Brian's brother, she decided.

It was a woman who stepped from the driver's seat, however, a very beautiful woman wearing a bleached white mink jacket over braided slacks. She had a matching white mink cap on her head and golden jewelry on an arm. Her hair was reddish, worn rather long.

"Brian! Darling!" she called.

He turned toward her, lifting a hand and waving it.

From where she sat unobserved in the dark Granada, Cherie saw the woman run to Brian, fling her arms about him, and kiss him. Brian, Cherie also noted, put his arms around her, hugging her.

Jealousy flared in Cherie. Who was this hussy who threw herself at Brian Cutler? She was honest enough to see that the woman was very beautiful, she had almost perfect features and was obviously wealthy. Her voice, too, was lovely, deeply musical.

"Where've you been, you naughty boy? I've been hunting all over for you! There's going to be a dance this weekend and I wanted to make sure you'd take me."

"Cara, I can't. There's business to attend to."

"On Saturday night?"

"There's a client I have. I have to be with her at all times. I can't tell you about it now. It's very much hush-hush."

Well, at least he was making mysteries for this one, too. Cherie saw her face cloud over.

"Oh, come on, Brian! You have to be with her *all* the time?"

"That's about the size of it." He looked back at the car

and Cherie saw the other woman glance her way, too—then stiffen.

"Here she is, Cara. Come meet her." His hand on her arm practically dragged the woman toward the Granada.

"This is Cherie Marsan, Cara. Cherie, meet Cara Slagle."

There was a little silence. Then Cherie smiled and said, "Happy to know you."

"Of course," said Cara Slagle, with ice in her voice. Then she turned toward Brian. "Is this your business? Is this the woman you have to stay with—even on Saturday night?"

Cherie grinned to herself. Let him wriggle out of that one.

Brian spread his hands. "Cara, it's true. Someone has already tried to kill her. Twice."

The redheaded woman looked at Cherie, and Cherie could almost hear her think: Too bad they didn't succeed.

Brian went on. "Come on in and have a cocktail. It isn't all that late. We were going to have a late supper. Join us."

Cara Slagle hesitated. "I'll come in for a quick drink, darling. But then I do have to run."

Brian came around and opened the car door. Cherie stepped out, very much aware that Cara Slagle was eyeing her up and down, taking in her clothes, her lack of makeup. There was almost a sneer on her ripe, red mouth. For a moment, Cherie didn't blame her. She looked like somebody's poor cousin. At least, compared to Cara Slagle.

She walked with Brian on her left, with Cara Slagle on his left, into the house. Cherie was determined not to let this other woman be alone with Brian for an instant. She didn't trust her one little bit. Yet why should she feel so strongly? Brian Cutler didn't mean anything to her. Just the same, she didn't like Cara Slagle.

And so, as they entered the house, she put her arm through Brian's, saying, "Come along, dear. Let's make those cocktails."

She caught Cara's swift intake of breath and was pleased with herself. Her arm in Brian's—actually, she had quite an armlock on him—brought him beside her to the mahogany bar in one corner of the downstairs den. Cara

came after them, and Cherie fancied that she could hear
Cara gritting her teeth.

"A martini for you, Cara," Brian was saying. "I'll have
one too, I imagine." He looked at Cherie, a question in his
eyes.

"Just wine," Cherie said sweetly. Then she added, looking right at Cara, "I find martinis dull the senses. A little
wine just helps you feel everything—more intensely."

She let her eyes wander at Brian as she said this, and
her smile grew dreamy. Cara was seething, she knew.

As she accepted her cocktail from him, Cara put her
hand on Brian's, smiling up at him. "I wanted to be the
first to congratulate you on the Emerson trial, darling. I
heard all about it, how marvelous you were with the jury."
Her eyes flashed at Cherie. "You're too good a lawyer to
take on cases that don't amount to anything."

Cherie winced. Maybe Cara Slagle was right, after all.
Who was she to take up Brian's time the way she was doing? A nothing. She didn't have any white mink jackets to
wear, no Continentals to drive around in. Misery flooded
up inside her.

Then Brian said, with a laugh in his voice. "Cara,
Cherie's case is the most important one I ever handled. Believe me!"

Cherie could have run over to him and kissed him. She
was aware that Cara Slagle was glancing at her in something like puzzlement, scanning her from head to toe and
wondering what was so important about her. Well, she was
just as puzzled as this woman. She would have died right
there and then, rather than admit it, however.

Instead she smiled at Cara Slagle, a secretive smile that
was meant to tell her that she and Brian had secrets they
were not going to share with anyone.

Cara asked, "Must you nursemaid her, Brian? Can it be
that important?"

"It is. She is. I can't let her out of my sight."

"Oh?"

Anger grew in Cara Slagle, glinting from her eyes. In a
way, Cherie didn't blame her. Apparently she considered
Brian Cutler to belong to her, and to find this—what was
the term she had used?—yes, this nobody occupying her
boyfriend's time to the exclusion of everything else was ex-
tremely disturbing.

Cara asked, "Am I never to see you again? Is that what you're trying to tell me?"

"Oh, Cara. Certainly not. Just for a few more days. That's all it will take. Then I'll be free as a bird again."

Oh, yeah? Cherie thought.

Cara Slagle beamed at him, stepping close to Brian, putting her arm about his neck, drawing his head down to kiss him. Cherie glared. It went on a little, that kiss—and Brian didn't seem too reluctant. Cherie cleared her throat.

She didn't like standing here while that woman kissed Brian. She didn't like it one little bit. Common sense told her she had no reason to protest, she certainly had no claim on him. But she could not help the fury that rose up inside her, the flash of an almost savage anger.

She had to restrain herself from leaping forward and pulling them apart. Oh, but he was going to pay for this! She did not know how, but he would. She would see to that!

Then Cara was patting Brian's cheek with her soft palm, looking up at him adoringly, saying, "I really have to run, you naughty boy. Thanks for the drink, I really needed it."

Her eyes touched Cherie gloatingly, then slid past her, as though dismissing her. She gathered up her purse and gloves and then tucked her arm through Brian's.

"See me to the door, pet."

Cherie glowered, left alone. She'd bet that woman was hugging and kissing Brian out there at the front door. Where was his brother? Why didn't he show up and put a stop to this? Why didn't she, for that matter?

I have no right. Brian Cutler doesn't belong to me.

She tilted her glass and finished the wine in one gulp. A moment later, the front door closed and she heard a car engine start. Then Brian was coming back into the room, smiling all over his face. There was lipstick on his mouth.

"You're disgusting," Cherie said. "Lipstick all over you."

"Is there?"

He didn't have to act so innocent, looking blankly at her as he drew out his handkerchief and began wiping. When he was finished, he grinned at her. "Cara's very affectionate. It's nice in a girl to be affectionate, isn't it?"

I ought to belt him! she told herself, seething. Affectionate? Ha! Like a hungry tigress. All that one wanted was Brian Cutler. And if somebody didn't interfere, she was going to get him, too. Serve him right, of course. Didn't the big ninny see what that woman wanted? Or didn't he care?

"I seem to recall your telling me that you couldn't recall the last girl you kissed. What a joke. Obviously, it was that one, wasn't it?"

"We-ell, yes. I think it was."

Her sneer was very obvious. "I suppose you enjoyed it, too?"

Brian glanced at her, opened his lips to speak, but closed them again rather quickly. "She's very affectionate," he murmured.

"Will you stop telling me how affectionate she is?" she yelled. "I think she's just a coldhearted bitch!"

"What do you feel like for dinner?" he asked abruptly. "I think there's some cold chicken in the refrigerator. We could have that, or make sandwiches."

"Stop changing the subject. We were talking about you and that woman."

"Oh, we're just friends. That's all."

"Ha! Some friends. Kissing cousins, I suppose."

"No." Brian shook his head. "We're not related."

She swung. She could not help it. Something came up inside her and made her do it. Her palm landed hard against his cheek, and the sound of the blow was loud.

"Ohhh," she wailed, "I didn't mean—"

That was when he grabbed her, yanked her up against him with his arms around her, and began kissing her. His kisses were hard, furious; there was rage in them—but there was something other than mere anger, too. Cherie could feel that other emotion, all the way down to her toes.

She didn't know how long the kissing went on. Five minutes? Ten? She was never afterward certain. But when he let her go, when he held her at arm's length and stared down at her, she knew she was still floating in a very happy cloud.

"Why did you make me do that?" he bellowed.

She blinked up at him. "Do what?"

"Kiss you like that."

"Didn't you want to?"

"Certainly I wanted to! That's the most stupid question you've ever asked me."

"Well, then? If you wanted to, you did." She grinned up at him, moving closer. "You want to go on kissing me?"

"I most certainly do not." He ran his fingers through his hair. "I don't make a habit of kissing girls, despite what you seem to believe. It's just that you hit me and I lost control of myself."

I ought to hit him again. I liked his kissing me.

In a dreamy voice, she said. "It's fun to lose control of yourself at times, isn't it?"

He glowered at her. "You're my client. I can't make a habit of kissing my clients this way."

"Indeed not," she agreed. Then with an impish smile, she added, "Just me."

Brian threw up his hands. "Come on into the kitchen. The servants have all gone home. We'll have to scrounge around and serve ourselves."

He caught her hand and almost dragged her with him, though Cherie told herself she was going very willingly. Her heart was singing a little song inside her, and she felt wonderful. She wondered fleetingly if she could be in love.

No, of course not. She was not a person who fell in love. Still, nobody had ever made her feel quite this way before. Happy and uncaring about anything except being with Brian. Ready to fight to keep anyone else from kissing him. She thought angrily of Cara Slagle. He would have to stop kissing that one. Indeed, yes. He would have to stop her from kissing him, too.

From now on, she was the only woman who was going to kiss Brian Cutler. Or know the reason why!

In the kitchen, she pushed him out of the way and went to the huge refrigerator. There was cold chicken in there, carefully covered. There were some cold, peeled potatoes, too. She could hash-brown those, with a couple of onions.

"Sit down," she told him. "I'll cook the supper."

She began to hum as she went about her preparations. It came to her as she worked that she had never before cooked a meal for a man other than her father.

It was a good feeling.

7

The meal she prepared was a good one, Cherie thought, everything considered. She noticed that Brian ate with relish, diving into the plate she had heaped high. There was a warm feeling in her heart as she regarded him (when he wasn't looking at her), and she decided it was fun to cook for him. Odd, she had never felt that way about anyone else.

When they were finished eating, she poured hot coffee.

It was then that Brian said, "Tomorrow when we go to see those lawyers, I don't want you to say a thing—unless I ask you something, of course."

Cherie tilted her chin. "What lawyers? And why shouldn't I speak?"

"The lawyers are Regan, Hennessey, and LeBlanc. The reason why I don't want you to open your mouth is because I'm afraid you'll prejudice yourself."

She frowned. "Prejudice myself? What does that mean?"

Brian grinned. "I guess you could call it legal talk for not putting your foot in your mouth." He reached out, caught and held her hand. "Just promise me, will you?"

"Oh, all right. I'll be like a regular dummy."

"Good girl. Leave it all to me."

Cherie sighed. "I wish I knew what it was I was leaving to you. I feel like somebody in a pitch-black room, stumbling around, not knowing where I'm going—or even where I've been."

Brian chuckled. "Just stay that way and everything will be fine."

She put her elbows on the table and leaned her chin on her folded hands. She stared right at him, and she asked slowly. "What is this 'everything,' Brian? Oh, I know you're doing something for me—something great, for all I know. But that's the whole trouble. I don't know. Not a thing."

Brian finished his coffee, rose to get a second cup. When he was seated again, he said slowly, "I'm bucking powerful forces, Cherie. I'm going up against a battery of legal brains that are the pride of the Louisiana bar." He smiled wryly. "All for you, too. So don't you fight me."

"Who's fighting? All I'm doing is asking."

"Tomorrow. You'll learn everything tomorrow."

He looked vaguely worried as he said that, and Cherie wondered if he himself might be in danger, as she apparently was. A stab of chilling fear stabbed into her. She didn't want anything to happen to him! She could not explain what it was she felt, but she knew very well that if anything had happened to Brian Cutler, she would just about die.

She smiled faintly. "All right. You're the boss. I'll do whatever you tell me to do. I won't make waves. Fair enough?"

"I couldn't ask anything more. Now get upstairs and into bed, please. We have a very busy day tomorrow. I want you at your best."

"Sure. After I do the dishes."

"The servants will do them tomorrow. I'll just stack them in the sink and leave them."

Cherie stood up. She had never had any servants, of course, and it seemed not quite the thing to do, to leave all this work for them. But Brian was at her elbow, turning her away, walking her toward the hall and the big staircase.

"Get a good night's sleep," he told her.

She trudged up the stairs, wondering what in the world Brian was getting her into. Obviously, he was counting on the fact that she was not a Marsan—but somebody else. Ah, but who? What was so important about who she was? A waif, she had been when the Marsans took her and brought her up. She was no more than that now, except that she was grown up.

As she undressed, she thought about her mother, that woman who had been crouched on the Marsans' doorstep with her in her arms. Who had she been, that woman? She had come out of the night and the storm like a ghost, without a name, with nothing but a lot of money in her pocket.

In her pajamas, Cherie stared at her mirrored reflection. "Do I look like her? I know I look like that woman in the

painting in the Mannering house, but do I look like my
mother or my father? Or neither of them?"

She smiled wryly. "In other words—who am I?"

She crawled into bed and fell asleep.

Morning sunlight woke her very early. Just as she
opened her eyes, there was a knock on the door. "Up and
at 'em," Brian called. "Get dressed. I'll have your breakfast ready. The servants don't come this early."

"Big deal," she muttered, throwing back the bedclothes.
"A couple of cups of coffee."

She looked at the clothes she had worn yesterday and
sighed. They would have to do. They were the best things
she owned. So what if Brian had already seen them. He
knows I'm a pauper.

Cherie dressed and ran downstairs. Brian was setting
softboiled eggs before her chair, together with orange juice
and coffee. "Eat," he told her. "I want you strong."

Cherie made a face. "I don't eat breakfast, I drink it."

Still! As she seated herself and reached for the orange
juice, she told herself that maybe she could nibble a little.
It certainly wouldn't hurt her. To her surprise, she ate everything that he had prepared for her, and drank three
cups of coffee.

Brain grinned at her. "There. Now you're ready for the
day."

"Hey, that's right. Today I solve the mystery." She
glanced at him inquiringly. "Time to tell me? No, not yet.
I can see that by your face. Okay. I'll wait."

He reached out and squeezed her hand. "Good girl.
Now come along. We have to go to my office."

"Your office?"

"Papers for you to sign."

Oh! Well, she guessed that would be okay. A lawyer al-
ways had his client signing all sorts of things, didn't he?
She went with Brian to the front door and out to his car.
She was very quiet, she didn't talk for a long time.

Finally Brian said to her, "Cat got your tongue?"

"I'm doing what you told me to do. Keeping my mouth
shut."

He laughed. "Guess I asked for that. You can talk to
me, though."

"No." She shook her head firmly. "If I talk, we'll fight. I
don't want that."

His office was in a huge building on Earhart Boulevard.

She walked with him from the parking lot to the elevator and rode up several stories. Then he ushered her into a reception room, the walls of which were huge with paintings, and where a middle-aged woman was sitting at a desk. At sight of Brian, the woman sprang to her feet.

"The papers are ready, Mr. Cutler." She smiled and looked hard at Cherie.

There was something about the way she regarded her that disturbed Cherie. She could not make out what it was in the woman that surprised her. Awe? Well, hardly. Jealousy? No, it wasn't that. Cherie glanced back over her shoulder as she followed Brian into a hallway. The woman was still staring after her, still with the same expression on her face.

"This way," Brian said, and brought her into a large room fitted out with a desk and some chairs. There were pictures on the walls, flowers in jardinieres, and the windows looked out over the city.

She saw papers arranged on an otherwise spotless desk. She sank into a chair as Brian seated himself behind the desk and began to look over those papers. He was all business now, Cherie noted. His eyes scanned the typing; he read swiftly, competently.

Then he folded back some of the papers and showed her the last page. "Sign here, please." He smiled.

Cherie scowled. "Don't I even get to read what it is I'm signing?"

"Sure, if you want to."

She eyed him a moment, then shrugged. "I'll sign. I know you have my best interests at heart."

He busied himself for a few moments, then stood up, reaching for a briefcase and slipping the papers she had signed into it. "All right. Now we can go."

"Go where?"

"Down three flights to the offices of Regan, Hennessey, and LeBlanc. They're in this building. Makes it easy, doesn't it?"

The offices of Regan, Hennessey, and LeBlanc were just as large, just as imposing, as those of Cutler and Cutler. The receptionist was younger, prettier, and she didn't stare at Cherie as the other one had done. She reached for a phone when Brian appeared and spoke into it.

A moment later a man in his early forties stepped from a doorway into the room, smiling a greeting at Brian even as he advanced with outstretched hand. His eyes slid sideways at Cherie and she saw them widen suddenly, as though in recognition.

Everybody seems to know who I am except me.

"Come in, come in," he said to them, standing to one side and ushering them into a hall with an outstretched arm. Then to Brian he murmured, "I wouldn't believe it if I hadn't seen that painting. I'm glad you phoned me, Brian."

When they were in a room fitted out with desk and several chairs, together with a couple of file cabinets, Brian opened his briefcase, lifted out the papers Cherie had signed, and handed them to Charles LeBlanc. LeBlanc scanned the papers, reading them rapidly. Then he dropped them on the desk and stared at Cherie.

He cleared his throat, then turned to Brian. "From what you've given me, from what I've seen of your client, I'd say you had an airtight case."

Cherie frowned. Airtight case about what?

Brian grinned, glancing at her. "She doesn't know a thing, Charley. I've deliberately kept her in the dark."

Charles LeBlanc said softly, "This won't be taken lightly, you know. The Mannerings aren't going to fold up and blow away. You may have a tough legal battle on your hands."

Brian nodded. "Of course. I'm ready. There's just one thing I feel you ought to know. Somebody's tried to kill my client—twice."

The older lawyer straightened, shocked. "Kill her?"

Brian told him about the attempt to gas her in her little apartment, about the car that had almost caused them to crash. He added, "I'm not letting her out of my sight. I want you to know that. If you can pass along a word, I'd appreciate it."

"By all means. I'll give it my prompt attention. This is reprehensible."

Brian spread his hands. "I have no proof. If I had, I'd go to the police. But you can just tell those two Mannering cousins that if anything happens to Cherie, I'll devote my life to seeing that they pay!"

Charles LeBlanc looked hard at Brian. "You suspect them, eh?"

"Wouldn't you? They have the best claim to the estate—until now."

The older man nodded heavily, very thoughtful.

Cherie sat quietly, looking at one man, then the other. She still wasn't at all sure of what was going on. Of course, it had something to do with an estate—whose, she had no idea—and to the Mannerings, who were somebody's cousins. What she had to do with all this, she had no idea.

Brian had told her that she would know what was going on, today. As yet, he hadn't opened his mouth. But he was going to tell her. Oh, my, yes. She would pester him until he agreed.

Then she sat very still, listening.

". . . best thing you could do is take her away somewhere. I don't know where, but someplace where nobody can find her. That's what I would advise."

Brian nodded, his face very serious. "I think you're right, Charley. I'll do that. Today. Then I'll be in touch, later on."

Take who away? Cherie thought. Where? Why?

Brian was standing, leaning across the big desk and shaking hands with Charles LeBlanc. Cherie rose to her feet, smiling at the older man, regarding Brian quizzically. Then his hand was on her elbow and he was turning her, taking her toward the door.

They walked down the hall together, Brian glancing at her almost wonderingly. Only when they were in the hall near the elevators, did she turn on him.

"I suppose you know what you're doing," she said. "I was quiet in there, I've been quiet all morning as I promised. Now can you tell me what's going on? And who are you going to hide?"

Brian's mouth opened and closed. "You mean you don't know yet? But I thought— Hey, you've got to be kidding! Don't you know what I just did?"

"How can I?" she howled. "I signed a paper, I went with you to see a lawyer, and you tell me I ought to know what's going on."

"I don't believe it," he muttered. He caught her elbow and guided her into the elevator. "Let's go get a cup of coffee and I'll explain it to you in words of one syllable."

"No need for sarcasm," she snapped. "I'm no lawyer. I don't know what you're doing."

He chuckled. "I'm about to make you the richest woman in Louisiana."

Cherie gasped. She pulled her elbow from his hand and said, "There's no need to insult me! I know I'm p-poor, b-but I've always h-had to do for myself and—"

"Oh, my God," he breathed. "Hey!"

Tears came down her cheeks. Fortunately they were alone in the elevator and nobody could see her but Brian. Cherie sobbed, aware that he was putting both his arms about her and holding her. She guessed he was only poking fun at her, he really didn't mean to insult her.

He had a handkerchief in his hand with which he was wiping her cheeks and staring down into her eyes as though he had committed some awful crime. "Please! No more tears! Please!"

"I ca-can't help it," she wailed.

"I thought you knew. Or guessed. I wanted it to be a surprise. A pleasant surprise. But this is awful!"

The elevator stopped, the doors opened. People were standing in the lobby, staring at them, waiting to get on. Brian put his arm behind her and practically carried her into the lobby.

I'll bet they think we're having a lovers' quarrel, Cherie thought wildly. She sniffed as she walked beside Brian, trying to get her emotions back under control.

They came out on the sidewalk and Brian hurried her along it. "Are you all right? How about some coffee? I know a nice little place not too far away."

"All right." She nodded. "Coffee sounds good."

When they were seated, Brian told the waitress, *"Beignets* and *café au lait,* please."

Then he put his hand on hers. "Cherie, I'm sorry. I didn't want it to be like this. I thought you'd understand as soon as we began talking with that lawyer."

"Understand what?"

"What I was doing. Filing claim for you to the estate of Josiah Mannering."

He sat back and grinned at her. Cherie shook her head. "I must be pretty dense this morning. Filing a claim? For me? To—to the estate of that man who died? The man who owned that magnificent house we went to? What was its name? Oak Haven?"

"That's it. That house, all his stocks and bonds, his oil wells, his various shipping interests, will soon be yours."

She could not speak. She sat there staring back at him, trying to understand what it was he had been telling her.

Then she burst out with "You're crazy! I always knew it. You're absolutely insane!"

"Oh, no, I'm not," he said quietly.

The waitress was there with the *beignets*—French doughnuts liberally sprinkled with sugar—and their *café au lait*. Cherie waited until she had gone, then she leaned forward.

"Are you trying to tell me that I'm going to be a rich woman?"

"That's it. Not just rich. Fabulously rich. You'll be a billionairess."

Cherie hooted. "I don't know what you're trying to pull, Brian Cutler, but whatever it is, it won't work." She reached out for a *beignet* and began chewing, glaring at him all the time.

Brian nodded. "So rich you won't know what to do with all your money. That's how wealthy you're going to be. You'll be written up in the papers, you'll have to hire a battery of accountants and lawyers just to tell you what it is you own."

"Phooey!"

Brian laughed. "I suppose it is pretty hard to understand, but I'm telling you the truth." He hunched forward, very intent, his eyes hard. "Why do you think those men tried to kill you? Not because you're Cherie Marsan—but because you're Clarissa Theresa Mannering."

"Come off it."

He shook his head. "I'm not kidding. That's who you are. Josiah Mannering's little lost grandchild, all grown up."

"I don't believe it. This is just some sort of game you're playing with me."

"All right. Let's suppose it is a game. Why in the world would I be playing it? And do you think Charley LeBlanc is in on it, too?"

Hmmmm. There was something to that. She could not imagine that older man playing any such trick on her. He was too dignified. If this were some sort of scheme of Brian's to seduce her, it was pretty farfetched. Besides, she told herself, he didn't really have to go to all that trouble. If he knew more about women, he would know she was just about ready to fall into his arms right now.

She chewed another *beignet*, scowling. This was ridiculous. All she was, was an artist, and maybe not a very good one, judging by her few sales. She sneaked a look at Brian. He seemed serious enough. She just couldn't understand what it was he had in mind.

An heiress! Me? Nonsense.

Just the same, he did seem to mean what he said. Cherie asked in a small voice, "What was that name you mentioned before? That you said was my name?"

"Clarissa Theresa Mannering. Old Josiah's granddaughter. Your mother, who left you with the Marsans, was married to Josiah's only son, John. Her name was Mildred Theresa."

"How can you know all that?"

"It's been public property for years. Old Josiah was in Europe when his daughter-in-law disappeared with his granddaughter, twenty years ago. He searched for her, he spent a small fortune in that search. Everybody in New Orleans knew about it. Nobody ever found you, until I did."

She sipped the *café au lait*.

Cherie shook her head. "I can't believe it. I don't believe it."

Quietly he said, "You saw that painting in the mansion. It's you. Oh, you're a Mannering, all right. I remembered that painting. When I saw you for the first time beside your oils near the cathedral railing, I recognized you. What I mean is, I saw your resemblance to Lavinia Mannering."

He spread his hands. "It couldn't be coincidence. It just couldn't. You had to be the long-lost heiress. That's why I took you to the Marsans. I hoped they might have some papers, anything at all that might prove you to be Clarissa Mannering."

Brian shrugged. "They didn't, but I'm not giving up hope. I'm going to hunt for something that will prove you to be who you really are. I'm hoping I'll find it. Meanwhile, I'll have to keep you alive and well until you can come into your inheritance."

Cherie studied her hands. "It just doesn't seem possible, what you're telling me. I can't get it through my head."

"Don't bother. Just leave it to me."

Cherie nodded. "Well, that's what I've been doing, isn't it?" She smiled at him. "So far you've done all right. I never thought that—well, that this was what you wanted me to know, today. I still don't believe it."

"Believe it. While you're at it, try believing that somebody wants you very dead. At first guess, I'd say it was your cousins. If you died, they'd get the whole kit and caboodle."

Brian stood up and Cherie joined him. They walked to the front counter and he paid for their snack. They they walked out on the sidewalk and toward his car.

Cherie asked, "What are you getting out of all this?"

Brian grinned. "A hefty legal fee, I hope. Surely you wouldn't begrudge me a nice fat fee if I can prove you're going to inherit more than a billion dollars?"

"Of course not! I'll give you anything you ask."

She wondered if he would ask for her hand in marriage. Hmmm. That might make him out to be a fortune-hunter, and Cherie thought she knew enough about Brian to know that he would do anything to avoid being called that.

Cherie brooded. On one hand, she was too poor to marry him. On the other, he might think she was too rich. Phooey! Why couldn't none of this have happened? Ha! Then he would never have met her.

As they got in the Granada, Brian said, "We're going to run away, you and I. I have a little cottage out there in the bayous. We'll stay there for a while."

Cherie glanced at him. "Just the two of us?"

"You want to invite somebody else?"

She certainly did not! To have Brian all to herself somewhere, sharing a little cabin with him for a few days, even a couple of weeks, sounded like heaven. She smiled to her thoughts. That cabin might be safe for her, but she wasn't at all sure how safe it was for Brian Cutler. Especially with Cherie Marsan around all the time. Before he knew it, he might have to marry her.

Cherie giggled.

"What's that for?" he asked as he drove.

"Nothing. Just doing some thinking."

She thought about it all the way to the big mansion he called River View. He would have to pick up some things, she guessed, food and clothing, stuff like that. But the most important thing would be her.

She began to look forward to what lay ahead.

8

When they were in his home, Cherie wandered about while he went upstairs to pack a bag. Cherie thought about that. She ought to pack a bag, too, she supposed, making a wry face. She certainly didn't have very many clothes with her. Not that she owned all that many, come to think of it. But she had more than what she had brought with her to River View.

She spoke about it to Brian when he joined her. "Just a few things, that's all I want."

"Not a bad idea. You ought to pack your paints and stuff, too, while you're at it. Who knows? You might want to do an oil when you get bored with the fishing and loafing."

Maybe she might want to paint at that, Cherie told herself as they drove into New Orleans. She might even do that self-portrait he had wanted the first time he had seen her. Cherie thought about that, admitting that she could not think of any good reason why she should not do it. She would give it to him as a present, sort of like her share of the costs of the cabin.

Brian was paying all the bills, and it wasn't right. But she didn't have enough money to offer to pay her fair share. Still, if she ever did come into this inheritance he kept babbling about, she would see to it that he got a very good fee for his legal work. She smiled at her thoughts. He might even get himself a rich wife. She wondered if Brian Cutler wanted a wife.

Cherie scowled. By golly! She would see to it that he wanted a wife, all right, or she wasn't a woman. She might have to be careful about this, he was probably all filled up with notions about how the man did the proposing and supported the wife. Maybe he even had some crazy idea that a guy shouldn't marry a very rich girl.

She would have to change his mind about that. Yes, indeed.

At her apartment, she moved quickly here and there, stuffing clothes into a bag that she pulled out from under her bed. She didn't have too much to be selective about, she didn't own all that many clothes. But she had a tidbit or two that might open his eyes. Cherie began to hum.

When the bag was filled so much that she had to sit on it to lock it, she gathered up her paints and brushes, her palette, her easel. What money she had, she had always spent on paints and brushes, figuring that if there ever came a time when she had no cash, she could always go on working. Now she was glad she had. It would save her trips into the city to buy whatever it was she might run short of.

Then they were off, with the Granada filled to capacity with her things. Brian had raised his eyebrows when he saw what she intended to take with her, but he had voiced no objections.

"I didnt' leave very much behind," she murmured in a small voice. "Just a few things that aren't all that important."

"As long as you brought enough to keep you busy."

She glanced at him out of the corners of her eyes. "Aren't you going to keep busy, too?"

"I certainly am. But I have most of my stuff at the cottage already. I use it from time to time for weekend trips and for my summer vacations. It's nice to be able to run off to somewhere like that."

Cherie thought so, too, especially considering that she wanted to be all alone with Brian Cutler. "No neighbors?" she asked.

"Not very close by. It's in a rather remote spot. Oh, sure, there are Cajuns here and there. I know most of them. But when I go off by myself, I really want to be by myself."

He turned his head a moment and grinned at her. Cherie did not know quite how to take that grin. "You won't be by yourself now. I'll be with you."

"I have to keep you alive and healthy. Right."

She wished he didn't make it sound as if she were a pet dog that had to be kept groomed for showtime. She kicked at the floorboard angrily. Why didn't he take more interest in her as a woman, not so much as just an heiress? But he would have plenty of chances, back there in the bayous. She would make certain of that. Even if she had to fling herself at him.

"We have to stop and stock up with food," he remarked after a time. "Pretty soon, too, because once we're at the cabin, there aren't any stores anywhere near."

"I wish I could pay my share," she muttered.

"Hey! You just stay alive. That's all I want from you."

Oh, is it? Well, you are going to change your mind about that, and fast, Brian Cutler!

But she only smiled at him very sweetly.

She went in with him to the supermarket, and as she trailed him up one aisle and down another, she grew appalled at the amount of food he was buying. He had enough to feed an army. Maybe even two armies. Steaks, chops, cuts of beef, lamb, and pork, together with hams. Her eyes grew very wide.

She tugged at his sleeve. "How long do you figure on staying at this cabin, anyhow?" she whispered. "Or are you planning on having a lot of people in to help us eat all this stuff?"

Brian studied his purchases. "I am buying rather a lot, at that." He grinned. "Still, you can't tell how long it will be. Besides, I have a big freezer that's just about empty right now. Better buy some more eggs."

It took him an hour and a half to make his purchases, and about half an hour to find enough space in the Granada to put it all. Cherie helped him tug stuff out of the way, to repack the trunk. When they were done, it seemed to Cherie that she could hear the Granada moaning.

"I feel as though we were going away for a year," she said as Brian drove toward the road that would lead them deep into the bayou lands.

"It doesn't hurt to be prepared."

At least he wouldn't have to leave to go shopping, Cherie noted. She would have him all to herself. That Cara Slagle would be biting her nails and having conniptions if she knew about this. Cherie grinned slyly to herself.

They came into Bayou LaFourche country along a dirt road, past moss-hung trees that seemed to add to the mystery of this corner of the world. Oaks grew large here, together with mangrove shrubs and marsh grass. It was a desolate world, but one that was filled with its own beauty.

Towering cypress trees could be seen now, interspersed with pecan trees.

Cherie stared around her, vaguely alarmed. At night, this would be a strange and eerie place. She shivered a little and looked at Brian.

"It's scary," she murmured.

"That's because you're used to having people all around you. Sure, it's lonely, but there are houses and people clustering here and there. Joe and I bought the land after scouting around down here for a year or two. We like our privacy when we want to get away. We picked our spot and built our cottage and the boathouse, we even spread some lawn around when we cleared the land."

"Sounds like a nice place."

"We like it. We come here to fish, to loaf. Nobody bothers us, and we've made friends with the Cajuns who live around the bayou. They're used to seeing our boat, used to our visiting for a time. They even watch out for the place while we're away. Good people, the Cajuns."

"I don't know very much about them, actually."

"Then you'll learn."

She would have to, she decided, if she were going to be around Brian Cutler very much. A thought touched her mind. "Does that Cara friend of yours know these Cajuns?"

Brian chuckled. "She thinks she's too good for them. Funny thing about Cara. She's not a bad sort, actually, but she's very stuck-up. Thinks that just because she has money, people should bow down to her. People aren't like that. Not around here, anyhow."

Cherie thought about that. She would have a lot of money, if Brian did what he wanted to do. She guessed she would be richer than anybody else, almost. Of course, there was the Getty fortune, and the Rockefellers and the Fords, but she would be able to hold up her end if she got more than a billion dollars! The idea of all that much money appalled her.

"Brian, what will I do with it? All that money and property?"

He laughed. "Have a good time. You can have anything you want then."

Can I, Brian? Can I have you?

Well, why not? Cherie asked herself. Uneasily, she wondered about that. She didn't see Brian as the sort of man to whom a billion dollars would have any special appeal. He had enough money as it was, didn't he? Or could she be mistaken about him? Could he be a fortune-hunter, after all?

It made no never-mind. She wanted him and didn't care whether he was interested in the money that would be all hers. Well, not much, that is. He wasn't a complete idiot, was he? A billion dollars wouldn't mean that he wouldn't marry her, did it?

Ha! Here she was thinking about marriage and all Brian was thinking about was keeping her alive. Suppose something happened to her? Suppose those cousins—or whoever it was that wanted her dead—should kill her? Then she wouldn't get either Brian or the money.

It came to Cherie then that she didn't care so much about the money. That was like a dream. But Brian was real. He was sitting right beside her. And it was him she wanted.

He turned the car onto a dirt road and moved along it. Then the high marsh grass on either side fell away and she found herself staring at a pretty cottage, framed in a setting of neatly trimmed grass, with the bayou water a hundred feet away. On either side rose the cypress and the oak trees, festooned with moss, and straight ahead was the bayou water, with sunlight glinting on it.

Cherie stared, speechless.

"Like it?" Brian asked.

She nodded. "It's beautiful. Come on. I want to see it! We can unpack later."

She got out of the car, walked to Brian, and stood close beside him, just staring. It was lovely. The cottage was painted white, with red shutters and a red roof. It looked so cheerful! Cherie smiled. The windows all had tiny panes of glass that added to its attraction, and the door was a brilliant red with highly polished brass fittings.

"Show it to me," she said.

He caught her hand and drew her forward. The sun was warm, she could hear the cries of birds in the trees and from somewhere she heard a loud splash. New Orleans was far away from here, almost in another world. She told herself, as she stared around, that she could paint here, very easily!

Brian opened the door and stepped back.

Cherie went into a bright room with scatter rugs on the

floor and walnut chairs and a sofa, with a big fireplace fashioned out of old bricks, with bright chintz curtains. There was a welcome in this room, it seemed to her like a happy place. To her surprise, she saw lamps here and there, which would obviously run on electricity.

Brian caught her stare, grinning. "We have a big motor here that give us all the electricty we need. It was one of the first things Joe and I thought of. I guess we went overboard a little with this place, but we both agreed that we wanted it, and so we didn't mind spending some money to fix it up nicely."

"It's beautiful," she breathed.

"Come along. I'll show you your bedroom. There are three bedrooms, actually. One for Joe, one for me, one for any guests we might have. This one is yours."

He opened a door and Cherie stared. It was lovely, with a large walnut bed and bureau, an easy chair, a reading lamp beside the bed. Two large windows gave the room cross ventilation. The window draped with chintz, a bright yellow to match the bedspread.

"It's lovely," she whispered.

"Not so bad for a hideout, is it?"

She turned to him. "Brian, how safe are we here?"

"As safe as anywhere we can go. Nobody will find us here without trailing us. And nobody did that, believe me. I checked our rearview mirror all the way."

Cherie shivered. There was an undertone of anger in his voice, and she realized—almost for the first time, she decided—that Brian Cutler was not playing a game. He was deadly serious.

She stood very close to him, wishing he would put his arms around her. But he ignored her to say, "Come on, we've got to unload the car, put things away."

Cherie followed him out, picked up packages, and carried them into the kitchen. She paused to regard it, her arms still holding the heavy bags.

The stove was wood-burning, there was a big table with benches, there were cupboards and closets built into the walls and painted white and yellow. It was a homey place, and Cherie liked it immediately.

Brian took the bags from her arms. "I'll start up a fire in the stove so we can have lunch. You—"

Cherie shook her head. "No. We'll eat lunch out on the lawn. Just sandwiches. I want to breathe in all that wonderful air and sop up some sunshine." She smiled suddenly. "As a matter of fact, I'm going to put a swimsuit on and get some sun."

"After we clear out the car," Brian said. "First the work, then the play."

"But of course," Cherie agreed meekly. "What else?"

In her room, she began removing her clothes from the bag, hanging them up in the closet. Ruefully, she decided she didn't have many nice things, her jeans were paint-stained—though she did have a clean pair—and her dresses weren't anything to make another woman sit up and take notice.

She held up her two-piece bathing suit, regarding it critically. It was old, she had not worn it for a couple of years, and she began to wonder if those bra-cups would completely contain her. So what? The only one who would see would be Brian, and she wanted him to notice her as a woman, didn't she? Not just as a client, a future heiress? She surely did.

In moments, she was wriggling out of her clothes and into the suit. It was a close thing. The trunks were something more than skimpy and the brassiere part strained to hold her in. Cherie frowned, not at all certain if this was very smart, wearing this thing. She wanted him to notice her, not to rape her.

Unfortunately, it was the only swimsuit she owned. Cherie shrugged. She guessed she could fight him off. If she wanted to, that is.

She came out into the living room, feeling rather bare and exposed. Luckily, it was a warm day, the suit felt comfortable enough, even if it was a bit tight in places.

"Hey, wow!"

That was Brian, of course, right behind her. She turned slightly, seeing him in Jantzen trunks, looking very fit. His own skin was somewhat bronzed; he must come out here to suntan quite a lot. Beside him, she felt very white.

His eyes went over her, lingering here and there. Cherie felt a flush rising from her throat into her face. Well, she had asked for it, hadn't she, by putting this thing on?

Mutinously she said, "It's the only bathing suit I own."

"You're beautiful," he breathed.

She flushed even more, not quite daring to meet his eyes.

"I want to get some sun," she muttered.

"And you will. But don't get too much. Sunburns hurt."

He walked past her into the kitchen. Cherie looked after him. He could have stayed to look at her some more, couldn't he? She hadn't raised any fuss about the way he had stared at her. Phooey! He was probably hungry.

She padded into the kitchen, saying, "I'll make the sandwiches. Ham with mustard okay?"

"Fine. I'll fetch us something to drink."

She slapped ham on bread and added mustard, telling herself not to be a ninny. What did she expect the guy to do, attack her? Tell her of his undying love for her? Well, no. She would have been horrified if he had done either. Hmmm. Maybe she wouldn't have been horrified about that undying-love bit. But he had just about ignored her.

He came up from the little cellar where he had been putting meat into the freezers, carrying a thermos bottle. "Grape juice all right?"

When she nodded, he filled the thermos and capped it, then caught up two glasses. He paused with them in his hands to look at her.

His eyes ran over her swiftly, before he lifted them to look her in the face. Cherie caught her breath. There was a fire behind those black eyes of his, a fire that leaped from him to her. She felt that heat and her mouth went dry.

They stood like that, staring at each other, before Brian shook himself suddenly and said, almost harshly, "Let's get outside."

She trailed after him, telling herself that Brian liked her. Liked her? She was positive that he loved her. Nobody had ever looked at her the way he had just stared. If she had said anything he might have thrown her down on the kitchen floor.

Would she have objected? Cherie grinned lopsidedly. Probably not.

But he had not.

The sun was warm, almost hot. Brian spread a worn blanket on the grass close by the bank where the bayou waters lapped. Cherie knelt to draw out the four corners so that they would have plenty of blanket on which to sit. Then she stretched out, hands clasped behind her neck, and felt the sun bathing her in its heat.

She was very much aware of Brian, who lay beside her. Once, as he lay down, his hand had brushed her bare thigh. He had withdrawn it quickly, as if—as if that thigh were red-hot. It might be red-hot after baking in the sun for a while, but right now it was cool. There was no reason for him to act as though she had some sort of disease.

Hey, what was the matter with her? Did she want him to caress her?

Cherie reflected about that, and decided that that was just what she did want. Gently, of course, and with appropriate love words to tell her how much he desired her, how much he needed her.

Instead, the guy just lay there.

Cherie scowled before she remembered that scowling might give her wrinkles. She turned slightly so that her hip touched his. Instantly he moved away.

Ha! Did he think she was trying to seduce him? She opened her mouth to snap at him, but decided against it. She wrigged a little, moving farther away from him, instead.

They lay there for half an hour before Brian spoke. Then he said, "How about those sandwiches? I could eat a horse."

She opened her eyes. He was leaning over her, staring down into her eyes. He was not touching her, however, he was maintaining his distance, as though he were afraid of her.

"You! You're always hungry," she said.

"Well, not always. There are other things beside eating."

She wished he would not go on staring down at her that way. It did things to her. She wanted to look away but could not.

"What things?" she whispered.

He shook his head. "Better not ask me that. It isn't advisable."

"Why not?"

He sat up, then, turning away from her, staring out over the bayou waters. There was a little silence. Then he said, "Look. We're going to be all alone here, just the two of us, for maybe a couple of weeks. I'm not very strong."

Cherie sat up in alarm. "Not very strong? Are you sick?"

He gave her a disgusted look. "You know what I'm talking about. You and me, woman and man. Living together like this isn't going to be easy."

Her heart started banging. Now he was getting to the nitty-gritty. Behind his back, she smiled. "And I thought it was. Nothing to do but laze in the sun and go swimming, maybe do a little fishing. Why shouldn't it be easy?"

"You have to help me," he grated almost angrily.

"How can I help you?"

"But not wearing that bathing suit anymore. You must know it does things to me. Certainly you're woman enough to know that. I'm a healthy guy. It wouldn't take much to push me over the edge."

Cherie shook her head. "I still don't get it."

"Put some clothes on, will you?"

"How can I get a suntan if I'm wearing a lot of clothing?"

He turned to glance at her. Maybe he saw her little smile, because he scowled. "It isn't funny," he snapped. "I'm serious."

"Just ignore me."

Ha! You ignore me, buster, and I'll clobber you good!

He hung his head, as though fighting an inner battle. Cherie watched him through partially shut eyes, waiting. His fists were clenched, she noticed.

"I can't ignore you," he muttered at last. "I keep trying, but I can't!"

Good. At least he knew she was a woman. Cherie crept closer, putting a hand on his shoulder. She sensed his hard muscles, the little quiver that ran through his body.

"Think of me as a client," she whispered, leaning so close that her long yellow hair tickled his skin. "I'm just a girl you're helping. That's all."

His head shook. "I've told myself all that. It doesn't do any good. You have to keep away from me, understand? Keep your distance. You have to help me. I don't believe I'm strong enough without your help."

Now she lay her cheek against his shoulder, from behind. His skin was hot, just as hers was hot, from the Louisiana sun. Her lips were very close to that skin, all she had to do was turn her head and she would be kissing his flesh.

"Get away," he breathed.

"Why, Brian! I'm beginning to think you don't like me."

He swung about suddenly, catching at her arms. He swung so abruptly that he lost his balance and toppled

against her. Cherie fell backward onto the blanket and he
came down on top of her. For an instant their eyes locked
and she shivered deliciously at what she could read in
those black eyes.

9

He was going to kiss her. She knew it, deep inside her. The burning in those eyes was matching the fire inside her own flesh.

And then he pushed himself away.

Cherie stared up at him, not quite believing this. A muscle in his jaw was working, and his eyes stared out across the calm, still waters of the bayou. Anger swelled up inside her, but it was more than anger, it was scorn as well. Scorn for this man who wanted so desperately to kiss her—and did not.

"What's the matter with me?" she yelled. "Have I got some sort of disease or something?"

He shook his head, not answering her.

Cherie fought to control her fury. Maybe she wasn't being fair to him. "It's Cara, isn't it? You love her, so you don't want to have anything to do with me." She added maliciously, "Other than as a client, that is."

"That isn't so! Cara's just a friend."

"Ha!"

He swung about on her, his face set and grim. But his eyes looked down at her, love for her swimming in their black depths. Ah, yes. She couldn't be mistaken about that.

"You have to help me," he whispered. "I told you before, I can't do it unless you give me a hand."

Cherie scowled. "I haven't the slightest idea of what you're talking about."

Brian seemed to erupt then. His hands came down on her bare skin, his lips caught her mouth and held it. Those big hands of his slid across her flesh, stroking it, and his mouth was something that seemed to eat at her. She was lifted upward, caught and held by his arms, and she began to tremble even as he was trembling.

She could hardly breathe. She felt her senses deserting

her, all but the sensation of exquisite delight. Something within her blossomed outward, exploding. She was moaning, though she wasn't aware that she was making those sounds. His arms were imprisoning her, holding her helpless, and she loved it.

Cherie squirmed closer, closer. Her own arms were about his neck, holding him. Their lips talked silently in that long kiss, moving gently, then fiercely. She thought for a moment she was going to die with this pleasure, it was almost too much for her to bear.

Against her trembling mouth he whispered, "Now you know. Now you understand. I can't help myself where you're concerned. So, you've got to be strong for both of us."

"Who wants to be strong?" she whispered.

"You do. You must!"

"Why?"

Brian groaned. "Damn it, you're going to be the richest woman in the state, maybe in the whole Southland. You can't afford to bother with me. Can't you understand that?"

"All I know is, I want you to go on kissing me."

Her arms tugged him down to her lips again. He tried to pull away, but she was too strong. Either that or he wasn't putting up much of a fight. Maybe the guy wanted to be convinced. Well, she was the one who would do the convincing, all right. She was going to make sure he understood that they loved each other.

He kissed her again, hungrily.

For a long time, they lay like that, kissing. Now his lips were on her mouth, now on her cheek, her throat, her forehead, her eyes. Cherie lay and reveled in the pleasure he was bringing her. The hell with that billion dollars! What was money compared to this? All she wanted was Brian in her arms, as he was now.

He was whispering to her as he kissed her, words of devotion, of love, of passion. She listened to those words, she caught them and put them in her heart and memory, eyes closed and lips smiling—when they weren't kissing him, that is.

Then he was pulling away from her, getting to his feet, walking to the edge of the bayou waters and staring down at them. Cherie lifted herself to an elbow, looking after him. What was the matter with the guy?

She rose upward, moved toward him.

Either he heard her or he sensed that she was coming toward him, for he whirled and lifted his hands, palms toward her. "Stay away. Please!"

Cherie smiled at him. "Why, Brian?"

He looked miserable. "Don't you understand? You're my client! I've brought you here to protect you, not to make love to you."

"You silly. We're all alone here—"

He groaned at that, but she went on. "There's nobody around to bother us, to stop us from doing what we want."

"That's just it. There's nothing to stop us—except my conscience."

Cherie sighed. She guessed she just couldn't understand Brian Cutler. Any other guy would be leaping at her, tearing off her swimsuit to make love to her. But Brian was being held back by some sort of . . . what? Legal ethics? Was that it? Was there some sort of unwritten law for lawyers that prevented them from making love to their clients? Ha! If that were the case, he could marry her and then everything would be perfect.

"You could marry me," she said in a small voice.

He threw his hands high. "Oh, my God! And be branded a fortune-hunter! No, thanks."

Cherie yelled, "To hell with that fortune! I don't want it."

He was shocked, she knew. He stared at her, hardly seeming to breathe. He shook his head, saying, "You don't know what you're saying. I have to think for both of us. I have to be strong. Strong!"

He began to walk up and down the lawn, as though trying to work off the excitement that was still in him. Cherie thought that maybe she should walk, too, because her heart was still banging away and there was a weakness in her body that she had never before experienced. She sighed and began to take long steps.

After a time, she grew aware that he had stopped walking and was looking at her. She asked, "Well, what's the matter? Don't you think I need to relax, too?"

"This is never going to work out," he muttered. "I thought it was. I really did." He came across the grass to stand before her, catching and holding her hands. "You have to believe me, Cherie. I thought this was a great idea, getting you away to this place where you'd be safe. Safe! Sure, safe from those guys that want to kill you—but not safe from me. I'm a heel!"

"You're not a heel. You just don't realize how much we mean to each other."

He looked down at her, and smiled weakly. "Oh, I understand that very much. And it mustn't be, I tell you. You're a wealthy heiress. I'm only your lawyer."

"You're not only my lawyer! You're my friend and—"

She had almost said "—lover." Well, so what? That was what she wanted, wasn't it? Yes, and it was what Brian wanted, too. She was woman enough to know that. The thing she couldn't understand was his reluctance. Oh, sure. She knew what he was trying to tell her, with all that talk about attorney and client. But the hell with that.

Cherie sighed. "I suppose you're right. We have to be very careful when we're all alone like this, in such a remote place."

"That's exactly it. The temptation is too much. We have to guard against it. Both of us, I mean."

"You mean like this swimsuit?"

She stepped back and looked down at herself. Brian was looking, too. The suit really did leave an awful lot of her exposed. Almost all of her, as a matter of fact. But it was the only bathing suit she owned. She certainly wasn't going to smother herself in clothes, in this place, where the sun beat down so fiercely. Brian would just have to get used to it. Or look the other way.

He nodded, but his eyes were going all over her. Cherie grinned. Ha! She could have Brian Cutler anytime she wanted. She would find a way to overcome those stupid scruples of his. But not right now. She didn't want to scare the guy into taking her back to New Orleans.

"I'll just go lie down on my front," she murmured.

When she was settled on the blanket again, she saw Brian walking up and down. He's trying to tire himself out, she thought. So let him. She was going to doze in this hot afternoon sun. Her eyelids closed.

She woke from her sleep, to find that Brian was sitting beside her, leaning over her, rubbing suntan oil into her shoulders. His touch was gentle, soothing, so much so that she just wanted to lie here and be pampered. But a cool wind was moving across the Bayou LaFourche, evaporating some of the heat from the sun.

"How long was I asleep?" she murmured.

"About an hour. I was afraid you might get sunburned."

She turned over, lay back, and smiled at him. "Thanks, Brian. My skin does feel a little overcooked."

"I don't want you to suffer."

"What time is it?"

"A little after five. I thought we might have a cookout tonight, I got the charcoal ready in the outdoor grill. All I have to do is put a match to it. I figured steaks might be what we'd have. And a salad."

Cherie smiled. "I'll fix the salad. But not yet. I'm too comfortable to move."

Her eyelids closed. It was very pleasant here with Brian. It was like a tiny corner of heaven. Just the two of them, to have each other without anyone bothering them or interfering. She wondered what Brian and his brother did at night. There was no television set, she had noticed that. But it didn't matter. She would be happy just sitting with him.

In time, she stirred and sat up. The wind really was cool now. She would have to remember that, bring a jacket with her next time. It would feel good around her now.

Brian said, "You ready to go in? You can shower, change."

"Mmmmm. I guess so."

Her shoulders were a little sore, she decided under the shower. Might be a good idea to avoid the sun tomorrow. Or if she wanted to sunbathe, she would do so for only an hour. She could hear Brian moving around in the kitchen, getting out the steaks, the dishes. It would be fun to eat charcoal-grilled steaks. It had been a long time since she had.

She selected a pair of slacks and a light sweater to wear. Brian couldn't object to this combination, they covered her up pretty good. Of course, the sweater was a little tight, but he would have to get used to that. On second thought, she didn't want him to get used to it. She wanted him to go on noticing her body.

In the kitchen, she made the salad, crumbling some blue cheese and dousing the chicory and escarole with olive oil and vinegar. She tasted it, was satisfied. Brian was outside, she could see him through the window, watching the steaks. Her mouth began to water, and she realized she was hungry.

Funny about that. She had never been very hungry back in New Orleans. Of course, she had always eaten dinner at night, and maybe a sandwich in the middle of the day, but ever since she had been with Brian, she had been wolfing down her meals as though there were no tomorrow. Was that what love did to her? Ha! And they said people in love never wanted food.

She arranged the table, setting out the plates Brian had put to one side, adding steak knives and forks, the salad bowl. Then she went out to stand with Brian and watch the steaks cook.

"Tomorrow we'll go fishing," he told her. "It's quiet and peaceful out there in the bayou. Nobody around, just the sun and the water." He glanced down at her. "You'd better wear a blouse or a shirt or something to keep off the sun."

It was so wonderful, standing here with Brian, listening to him worry about her sunburn. No one had ever worried about her, except for her adoptive father and mother, of course, when she had been little. Cherie decided she liked it.

They ate the steaks and salad eagerly. Brian was a pretty good cook, she told herself. Especially with steaks on a charcoal fire. When they got married—if they did, that is—she would always let him do that chore.

Washing the dishes, stacking them, brought them an added intimacy. As though they really were husband and wife. As she hung up the towel with which he had been drying those dishes, she asked, "What do we do now?"

He grinned at her. "Read or take a walk. You have your choice."

I'd rather sit with you and have you kiss me, she thought, but she said, "No walking. I'm tired enough. You got any good books to read?"

They read side by side in the living room, with a small fire going in the fireplace. Just like old homebodies, she told herself. It was fun, though. Knowing Brian was so close to her she could reach out and touch him was very pleasant. From time to time she glanced at him—at those times when he wasn't looking at her. He looked at her a lot, she knew, and was pleased by it.

As she lay in bed that night, she knew that she could be very happy indeed if she could spend the rest of her life here in this cottage with Brian. It was all she had ever asked out of life, really.

Next day, Brian woke her with a cup of coffee. He was smiling down at her as he put the cup and saucer on the end table. "Thought you might like to have breakfast in bed."

"You'll spoil me."

"Just getting you used to being a rich girl."

She frowned at that after he had left to prepare his own breakfast. Was that how he saw her? As a spoiled woman, expecting everyone to wait on her, to fall down and adore her whenever she appeared? Cherie made a face. She was not like that, and in a way, she resented Brian thinking she would be.

Cherie tugged on the bathing suit, standing before her mirror and realizing that the angry red on her shoulders, back and sides—oh, yes, and on the backs of her thighs as well—was rather painful. Brian had appeared a little late with his suntan lotion. She winced as she moved.

Well, it really wouldn't matter, not in that boat today. She wouldn't have to move around, and her old shirt, which she had pulled on over the bra part of her swimsuit, ought to protect her. She walked out into the kitchen.

Brian had made sandwiches and filled two thermos bottles with coffee. He was busy now putting all of that into a container. He looked up as she entered.

"Got it all done. Thought you and I could have a second cup of coffee together. Sit down, I'll pour."

He was waiting on her, she realized, treating her just as though she were already the acknowledged heiress to that billion dollars. Cherie wasn't sure she liked that. All her life she had had to do for herself, and had become rather independent.

They drank their coffee, chatting idly about fishing. Cherie had gone with Pierre Marsan often enough, she knew what a pole and a hook were for. True, she had never fished in a bayou, but she supposed it was much the same thing. But as she followed Brian to the boat floating under its roofed shed, she did not see any fishing poles.

When she mentioned it to him, he laughed. "Not going out for fish, but for oysters and shrimp. The commercial fishermen get most of those, but I know a spot or two where we can find what we want."

He put some long poles in the boat, at which she stared.

Then, after he had helped her in, he untied a rope and sat down facing her. With an oar, he pushed the pirogue out into the bayou. Then he began to row.

Cherie studied him while pretending to take in the beauties of the bayou. In the shirt and the slacks he wore, she could sense his strong body. His muscles bulged and relaxed, there was delight in his eyes and happiness on his lips. He was a strong man, she realized. He seemed untiring as he sent the pirogue through the bayou waters, sliding along with hardly a ripple.

All around them was the silence of the bayou. The waters were still and deep, the marsh grass thick and luxuriant, the trees huge, festooned with moss. It was almost like a natural cathedral, she thought. They seemed to be closed off from the rest of the world. It was very calm, very soothing.

"We're after shrimp today," Brian said, stroking steadily. "The shrimp come up into the bayous from the gulf, as larvae. The tide sweeps them in and they make their homes in the underbrush where they feed and grow. Their tails enlarge. They go back into the gulf where they grow even larger.

He chuckled. "We aren't a shrimp boat, of course. All we want is enough for a meal or two. I'll prepare a sauce that will make them melt in your mouth. Oh, yes. A feast of shrimp is a treat you'll enjoy."

He moved the boat into more remote areas of the huge bayou, and headed it toward a fallen cypress tree. He put down the oars now and drew out a net that he fastened to the two poles. "These we will put down into the water and drag. You hold one. I'll grip the other."

He began to move the oar on his right side, slowly. The pirogue moved gracefully. Then he used the left oar. "We don't want to startle them or frighten them. Shrimp can escape us if they become alarmed."

The boat moved on, very slowly. It was delightful here; from time to time Cherie looked down into the waters, but she could see nothing in their depths. She felt the sun on her and it gave her a warm, cozy feeling. It was good to be here with Brian, helping him. It made her feel needed.

She glanced at him. Did he want to feel needed? She wondered about that. He was very independent, maybe he didn't want to be needed, by anyone. Mutinously she tilted her chin. She needed him. He must need her. He must!

Cherie did not know how long they took. She was enjoying herself too much to think about time. But at last Brian put down his oars and caught her pole as well as the one he held. At his direction, she took his place on the thwart.

He lifted the poles, sweeping them and the net between them toward the boat. She saw the muscles of his arms and back bulge. Then he was lifting the nets upward. They must have been heavy, he was straining.

"Let me help," she said, and came to stand at his side, gripping the far pole. She lifted, saw the net break water, filled with shrimp. Cherie cried out in surprise, the pole almost slid from her fingers.

She righted herself, lifted, watched as the net came up over the sides of the boat and poured its catch onto its floor. She was standing ankle-deep in shrimp, and she laughed, looking at Brian.

He was grinning at her. "A good catch. We'll eat shrimp for quite a while now." He added with a glance at her, "I hope you like them."

"Oh, I do."

Brian folded the net with the poles and put it down in the bottom of the pirogue. Then he sat down and began to row.

"There's a little place I want to show you," he told her. "It isn't far away. Joe and I used to come here when we were youngsters, and pitch a tent. It's quite an experience, staying in a tent in the heart of Bayou LaForche. It's quiet at night, except for the bellow of an alligator or the cry of a bird. It's almost like being alone in the world."

He rowed for a time and then the marsh grass and the trees seemed to fall away and they were in a tiny lake, or what seemed like a lake, and on the far side was a level stretch of grass. Cherie stared. It was cleared land, it was like a lawn there in the bayou. Brian rested on the oars, looking at it.

"Joe found it one day while out shrimping. He brought me to it, with a tent. We stayed overnight there a couple of times. Someday," he added wistfully, "I'd like to come here with the girl I love. You can see the stars everywhere in the sky when you look up at night. It's—well, it's elemental."

Cherie sat very still. With the girl he loved. Well, that was she, naturally. She scowled. Wasn't it? He wasn't say-

ing, but she herself had no doubts. How would she enjoy a
night here, with him in a tent, and the stars bright above
them?

I would love it! Wherever he was with me, I would love.

"What girl?" she muttered.

He chuckled. "Someone I loved, someone who loved
me. Someone—who wouldn't mind sleeping out at night
in a tent."

"What about Cara?"

His laugh was full-throated. "Cara? Forget it. She
wouldn't get in a pirogue to be rowed over here, and
there's no other way of getting here."

Cherie sat back, satisfied. She had clambered into the
pirogue, she had helped him catch all those shrimp. She
would love to share a tent with him underneath a sky
filled with stars. She sighed. Did the big idiot know that?
Would he ever go to the trouble of finding out? She
doubted it. He had her pegged as a spoiled, rich woman
who couldn't be bothered to soil her feet.

Ah, but that wasn't true. Hadn't she worked beside him
to catch all these shrimp? Hadn't she delighted in escaping
here with him, to all this solitude? If she were spoiled, she
would look down her nose at all this. How could he think
of her as spoiled? She'd had to paint and struggle to put a
few dollars in her purse. Spoiled? Me? Anger began to
mount in her.

She was opening her mouth to lash out at him when he
reached forward and caught her hand. "If things were different between us," he said wistfully, "I'd ask you to come
out here with me. It would be the most exciting thing I've
ever done."

Well, now. Maybe he was beginning to get some sense.

"I'd like that," she murmured. "I'd just love it."

His hand fell away and he shook his head. "It can never
be. I'm just being stupid." His smile was regretful. "Make
believe I didn't say that."

Oooooh! The man was infuriating!

Her foot lashed out, kicked his shin. "Oh," said Cherie
sweetly. "Make believe I didn't do that."

She glared at him as he winced and rubbed his ankle.

He met her eyes and their gazes locked. His hand
stopped its rubbing motion on his ankle. The boat floated
lazily under them. Cherie knew her heart was thumping
louder, that there was a weakness all through her body be-

cause of the way he was looking at her. Nor could she turn her gaze away from him.

"It would be heaven," he said softly. "Just you and me underneath the stars, all alone on that stretch of grass, with a tent to sleep in."

"I know," she whispered.

"But you're a rich heiress. I'm only your lawyer."

He lifted his hands to the oars and began to row. Cherie could have screamed. What was the matter with the guy? Didn't he have any red blood flowing around inside his body? He wouldn't even look at her as he worked with the oars.

Tears began to trickle from her eyes.

10

The hours fled away into days, and Cherie realized one morning that she was happier than she had ever been in all her life. As she lay in bed early one morning—the morning of the fifth day they had been here—she thought about the fun she had had with Brian, here in his cottage. It had been like a vacation, a time of laughter and enjoyment.

They had fished and shrimped, they had cooked their meals side by side, they had spent long afternoons just lazing in the sun. She had quite a tan now, her sunburn was all gone. She had never felt healthier. She was safe here, with Brian watching over her.

Safe? Yes, that was true enough, but Cherie wished that she was not quite all that safe. From him, naturally. Oh, she wanted to be safe from those men who wanted her dead. No doubt about that. But there were degrees of safety, weren't there?

For instance, why was she so safe from Brian himself?

Why couldn't he reach out and grab her and throw her down someplace, on a bed or a blanket out there on the lawn? And let things happen between them? Ha! Not him! He was like an old grandfather, concerned only with her health and comfort, her welfare.

Phooey! He didn't even try to kiss her. Or wrestle with her playfully. Still! If he did that, Cherie knew damn well what would happen. Oh, yes. She hugged herself and thought about that for a time. She sighed. Brian was never going to do anything about it. Not him!

Maybe it was her. Maybe he didn't like her enough to grab hold of her and to hell with the consequences. She scowled darkly at that thought. Could it be that he wasn't interested in her as a woman? Didn't she have enough—well, sex appeal to tempt him? Her scowl grew even blacker.

94

She got out of bed and moved toward the mirror. She was wearing a shortie nightgown, one that was a little tight on her. It was rather threadbare, too. It looked like a mist covering her body, and there were places where it didn't cover too much, at that.

Cherie grinned. If he saw her like this . . .

She shook her head so that her long golden hair flew. No! She was not going to parade around the cottage in front of him like this. There were limits to what a girl might do to get a guy.

Or—were there?

She could hear him moving about in the kitchen. He was starting the coffee, frying the bacon, getting their breakfast. Cherie thought for a time. Certainly there was no harm in going out there to get herself a cup of coffee and bringing it in here to sip while she got dressed.

Did she dare? She gave herself another look in the mirror, turning slightly, flushing as she realized how much this old short nightie was showing of her body. It wouldn't bother Brian, though. He was made of ice water. He wouldn't even give her a second glance.

She went and sat on the bed, waiting until she was certain that the coffee would be perked and ready to pour. Then she rose and moved in her bare feet toward the door of her bedroom.

She padded out into the kitchen, giving him a bright smile as he turned from the stove. "Coffee almost ready?" she asked. "I caught a whiff of it perking as I got up, and you know what?"

He was staring at her dumbly, his eyes going all over her. For a moment Cherie poised to turn and flee. She wasn't being fair to the guy. Then something inside her firmed and solidified. How fair was he being to her? She moved forward toward the stove, very much aware of how little her tiny nightie covered her.

"It smells great," she exclaimed.

Poor Brian! His eyes were big as saucers, they were eating at her as they stared. Cherie was delighted at what she read in his eyes. Oh, he wanted her, all right. There was no doubt about that. He was not indifferent to her, not at all.

"Could I have a cup?" She smiled up at him. "Just a cup to sip while I get dressed? Then I'll come out here and we'll have our breakfast together."

Was that a groan that came from him? She sure hoped so. Let him groan. Let him suffer. He was entirely too complacent to suit her. He was standing there with his arms at his sides, ignoring the frying bacon, ignoring everything but her.

Well, that was as it should be.

"A cup?" she reminded him.

Brian started. "Oh, a cup. Sure! I'll get it."

He brought it back, but the cup was making a tiny rattle in the saucer because his hand was shaking. Cherie hid a smile as she turned to lift the coffeepot.

"Maybe you'd better put it down on the table," she murmured.

He almost dropped it, doing as she asked. Cherie stepped closer to him, began to pour. She poured slowly, because she was enjoying this moment very much. The guy couldn't take his eyes off her. So let him look. So let him see what he was ignoring. He deserved to sweat just a little.

Cherie lifted her eyes and smiled up at him. "Thank you, Brian. I just couldn't resist coming out here for that coffee."

She put the pot back on the stove and turned to pick up the cup. That would give him an opportunity to take her in his arms and hold her. He just stood there, however, as though he were turned to wood. Cherie scowled faintly, lifting the cup.

Idiot! Didn't he know she was practically throwing herself at him?

She lifted the cup and carried the coffee back to her room. She slammed the door behind her and then stuck out her tongue at it. "You coward! You ninny! You scaredy-cat!"

Now the cup was rattling around on the saucer. She was so furious she was trembling. Cherie put it down and glowered at it. She had never before felt less like drinking coffee.

What was she going to do with the guy? How in the world was she ever going to get him to admit that he loved her, that he wanted her? He was always so cautious, so careful. Was that why he made a good lawyer? Cherie gritted her teeth.

She turned toward the bureau and pulled out her bathing suit. Not since the first day she had worn it here had she garbed herself in just the suit. Always she had worn a shirt with it. At first it had been to avoid too much sun, but lately she had been wearing it because Brian approved of it.

Cherie sneered. No wonder he approved of it. It hid her body from his eyes. Well, she wouldn't bother with a shirt today. It would be the swimsuit alone, with her in it. Or half out of it. Whichever way she wanted it. She slid from her shortie nightie. "And he won't make a move," she exclaimed bitterly.

Her eyes touched the coffee. She had not even tasted it. The hell with it! She carried the cup to the bathroom and dumped the coffee down the sink. Then she walked to the kitchen, a big smile on her face.

"That was delicious," she announced. "I think I could eat a horse."

He had turned from the stove where he was now frying eggs. He turned—and froze. His eyes widened as she grinned cheerfully at him.

"Aren't you . . . chilly?" he asked in a choking voice.

"On a hot day like this? Don't be silly."

She came and stood close beside him, wondering if he could smell the perfume she had put on. Casually she put a hand on his shoulder, which brought her even closer. Cherie smiled up at him.

"Don't let those eggs burn," she said. "You know you detest burned eggs."

He turned to the stove, began to lift the eggs onto plates where he had already put bacon. His hands were shaking, she noted with glee. So she did have some effect on him. Well, she had known that all along, of course. But it was nice to know she had not lost her touch.

As he put the plates on the table, she caught her chair and drew it closer to his, so that they were side by side. With innocence in her eyes, she said, "I feel like a cozy breakfast today."

Now she was darned sure he groaned.

Her leg nudged his from time to time as they ate. She would put her hand on his wrist casually, as she was talking. Always her eyes beamed at him. Oh, he was uncomfortable, she saw. Her nearness was disturbing him very much. Once when he tried to pull his chair away, she drew hers even closer.

Cherie was filled with laughter as she babbled on about

the day, about how lazy she had been, not painting lately, how glad she was that he had suggested they bring along her palette and easel and oils. Why, she might even begin painting this morning.

Brian answered her in monosyllables for the most part. He was paying an inordinate amount of attention to his food and coffee. He hardly lifted his eyes from his plate and cup.

Only when she mentioned her painting did he seem to take an interest. "That would be a great idea. Give you something to do."

And keep her out of his way, she told herself as she smiled at him. He was paying absolutely no attention to her, it was as though he had clamped a lid down on all his feelings, his emotions. There were times when she might hate Brian Cutler very easily, Cherie told herself.

Cherie glanced at him out of the corners of her eyes. His face was glum, he looked as though he were having very gloomy thoughts. Good! The gloomier the better.

"Yes," she said slowly, "I think I will get out my paints. I might do a bayou scene—or I might even do that self-portrait you wanted." Her eyes lifted as she looked at him. "You still want that self-portrait?"

"Of course I do," he enthused. "I think that's wonderful. How can I help? Oh, by carrying your things out to the lawn. And by staying out of your way."

Cherie sneered. Sure, run away and hide. Stay somewhere so you don't have to look at me, you coward. Irritated, she lifted her cup and dish and carried them to the sink. She was aware that he watched her from where he still sat at the table.

"Is anything wrong?" he asked.

She gritted her teeth. She would not answer him. She would not! For if she did, she would reveal a little of the anger that was eating in her. She had always possessed a temper, and she was very much aware that Brian Cutler was trying it as it had rarely been tested before. If he kept on, she would hurl one of these dirty dishes at him. She would!

She forced herself to turn slowly, made her lips grimace a smile at him. "Wrong? What could be wrong?"

His face was troubled. "I don't know. I thought we were getting along so well . . ."

Oh, you did, did you?

". . . that I wouldn't want anything to spoil it."

He looked so miserable, sitting there, that Cherie felt tears spring into her eyes. She hated to see him look like that, and hated herself for making him. Just the same, he was such an idiot that it was no wonder she got mad at him.

She forced herself to calmness. "Nothing's going to spoil it. Go ahead. Take my stuff out there on the lawn. Leave them there. I'll be out presently."

Cherie turned back to the dirty cups and dishes, and there were tears in her eyes. She did not want Brian to see them. She shook her head so that her long yellow hair tumbled down on either side of her face.

"If you're sure?"

"Yes, yes. Go on."

It wasn't unil he had left the house that she allowed herself to sob. Her head hung down and her tears dripped into the dirty dishwater. She wept silently, softly, telling herself that she didn't want that billion dollars, all she wanted was Brian Cutler. There was an ache in her body that he caused, and that only he could allay by holding her and telling her he loved her.

"Oh, damn," she muttered, brushing away the tears.

This was getting her nowhere. She might as well go out there and paint a picture. At least it would keep her busy, maybe even force her to think about something other than herself and Brian. Slowly she dried her hands.

What would she paint? The bayou? It would make a lovely setting for an oil. But she didn't feel like staring at a bayou, not in her present mood. She really didn't feel like painting anything. She was just forcing herself to do it, to keep busy.

She walked into the bedroom to fix her face, to remove all traces of her tears. As she stared at her reflection in the mirror, she recalled how Brian had wanted her to do a painting of herself.

"Why not?" she muttered. What difference did it make, anyhow?

From her purse she took out a small hand mirror and carried it with her to the easel that Brian had set up on the lawn. She propped it up, stared angrily into it. Her flushed, rebellious face stared back at her. Cherie stuck her tongue out at her reflection.

She ought to paint *that* picture!

Her sense of humor came to her rescue and she laughed. That would make a great work of art, wouldn't it? A picture of a girl sticking her tongue out at herself.

Ha! Why not?

She began to sketch out an outline with a bit of charcoal. But as she worked, she lost a little of her rage, told herself that Brian was doing all he could to help her, she was acting like a spoiled brat. And she had always hated spoiled brats. She would do a good picture of herself, a really good one.

A head-and-shoulders job. Sure. Then she would give it to him and let him moon over it. If he was afraid of the original, he might enjoy the copy.

She worked steadily, losing herself in her art. The charcoal image took shape beneath her gifted fingers. She used the charcoal lightly, with just a suggestion of what the final picture would look like.

She forced herself to smile, so that she might capture that smile. It wasn't a very cheery smile, though. No matter how she tried, the corners of her lips seemed to droop. She had to do better than that.

"Hey, how are we doing? Or shouldn't I disturb the artist?"

He had come up behind her so quietly that she had not heard him. Cherie turned to glance at him. He was so eager, so boylike, that she couldn't help it. She didn't want to, but she smiled back at him.

She caught a glimpse of that smile in her mirror. There! That was the smile she wanted. Quickly she sketched, forgetting all about Brian. Not until she was satisfied that she had captured what she wanted, did she turn again.

He was staring at her adoringly. His heart was right up there in his eyes, and Cherie felt her own heart respond to that look. A little corner of her mind asked her why he couldn't look at her that way all the time. Maybe he could. Maybe he was just afraid of her.

Now why should she think that? She was no ogress to eat him up, no female monster to claw at him. Far from it. She wanted to dissolve in his arms, to be kissed and petted and be told how wonderful she was, how beautiful. Could it be that he was afraid of all that wealth she would inherit?

Ah, that was stupid. Why would he be afraid of money?

"It's going to be a beautiful painting," he said softly.

"Oh, I don't know. I'm not sure I can paint all that beautifully."

"Sure you can! I've seen your work, you know. You're a terrific artist."

"Am I, Brian?" she asked wistfully.

"You kidding? I think you're marvelous."

"As a painter?"

"Yes, and as a person, too. I admire you tremendously."

That was nice, she thought. But was it only his admiration she wanted? A girl needed more than just cold admiration. She needed to be swept off her feet, fussed over, told that she was the only person in the whole world. The only person who could ever make Brian Cutler happy.

She realized with a start that they were staring at each other again, drowning in each other's eyes. She wanted this moment to go on and on, because she got the message his eyes were giving her, all right. It came through loud and clear. If only the rest of his body would act on what his eyes were saying!

He seemed to shake himself. "Here I am bothering you and I promised myself I wouldn't."

"It's all right. I don't mind."

"No, no. I know how the artistic temperament is. You mustn't have any distractions."

"I'm not that temperamental." She smiled.

"Just the same, I'd better run. I'm going out in the boat and leave you by yourself so you won't be interrupted again."

"We-ell, don't go far. I-I'll miss you."

He grinned. "I won't. I'll be close by."

She turned back to her painting, but not before she had watched him walk away to the boathouse. She lifted her palette, began to squeeze out oils. It was pleasant, painting here, knowing Brian was not far away. She nibbled at her lip and touched paint to the canvas.

She worked steadily, forgetting him, forgetting everything in her concentration. For a time, she seemed even to forget Brian. Yet he was never really out of her thoughts, for she was doing this picture for him. It would be her present to him. Naturally, then, it had to be perfect.

Slowly her image grew on the canvas. Her yellow hair seemed almost to glow; she fussed over her eyes, trying to make them as tender as she could, seeking to catch that happy smile on her lips. Time after time she went over what she had done, not being satisfied. She stood back and surveyed the canvas, shaking her head, telling herself that she would never capture that picture of her she had in her mind.

"How is it going?" Brian called from the boat as he stepped onshore.

Cherie walked toward him, rubbing a cloth over her fingers.

"I can't catch myself," she muttered. "It just isn't working."

He turned her, walked with her to the easel. He stood a moment, eyeing it, then swung on her. "Why, it's magnificent! You're just as lovely in oil as you are in the flesh. How can you say it isn't what you want?"

She eyed the painting again. It wasn't bad. As a picture, it was good enough. Maybe even very good. But it was not the Cherie Marsan she had visualized from somewhere deep inside her.

She shook her head. "I'm not happy with it."

"But—"

She lifted her hand to cover his mouth. "It isn't what I want," she told him gently. "But I'll work on it some more. I want it to be absolutely perfect."

He had raised his hands to catch her wrist. But instead of pulling away her hand, he was kissing its palm where it pressed against his mouth. Cherie felt those kisses, grew aware of the hunger in them.

Instead of her hand, he could be kissing her lips.

Very gently he drew her hand away, but held on to it. His eyes looked down into hers. "It is perfect," he said softly. "Just as you are perfect."

Well, now. This was more like it.

"You're just saying that."

"I mean it! I think you're the most beautiful girl I've ever known! As a matter of fact, you're so lovely you scare me."

"I am?" she asked dazedly. "I do?"

"Don't you know it? You've been staring into that mirror all day, practically, putting down on canvas what you've been looking at. Well, look at it again. Just study it. Aren't you beautiful?"

Her heart was pounding away at a great rate, but Cherie made herself look at the painting she had done. It didn't seem so beautiful to her. "It's just me," she murmured. "I mean—I."

He put his arms about her, drew her in against him. "I've been a fool," he said. "Here I've been thinking all along that you wouldn't do that picture of yourself because you thought you didn't look like Lavinia Mannering. Why, you're her double!"

Cherie stared up at him. Lavinia Mannering? Who was Lavinia Mannering? What did she have to do with it? For a moment she could not recall who that woman was. And then she remembered.

"That one," she snapped. "All pride and look-down-your-nose-at-other-people."

Brian chuckled. "She was accounted the most beautiful woman in all New Orleans in her day."

"So who cares?"

"I care, and so should you. Very much."

Her lower lip curled outward rebelliously. "Why should I care about her?"

Brian chuckled. "Sometimes I get the impression that you don't give a hoot about the billion dollars."

There were other things she'd give more hoots about. As a matter of fact, she was looking up at him right now. He was about to let his arms fall from around her, she sensed, so she crowded in a little closer to him.

"Money isn't everything," she muttered.

"Maybe, but it sure is a big help."

She eyed him closely. His arms were holding her once again, holding her rather tightly, she decided. And she liked it. Cherie murmured, "Tell me, Brian. If you had your choice between a girl you loved and a billion dollars, which would you choose?"

He laughed gently. "The girl, of course. Money can't cuddle up to you of nights, or sit across the table from you at dinnertime. Money can't talk to you, can't nestle close when you put your arms—Well, I guess you know what I mean."

"I think I do. Why not tell me some more?"

"What else is there to tell? A girl you love will be with you always, sharing your life, your victories, and, yes, your defeats. Money? What can that do? So you have it to spend. A man can work and make money. A girl isn't as easy to get."

Hmmm. That sounded encouraging.

He stared down into her eyes. "You can't hug money, not the way I'm hugging you, for instance. Money isn't warm and loving. Money isn't having breakfast with you, or going out in a pirogue together, or cuddling up in bed together with all the night before you."

Cherie decided it sounded better and better, what he was saying. All she had to do now was convince him she was the girl to do all that with, for the rest of his life.

11

Cherie lifted her arms and put them about his neck. She crowded in closer to him, bringing her body into full contact with him. Every nerve end she possessed was clamoring with delight, she practically tingled with pleasure from her head to her toes. At last he was going to know that she wanted him to hold her, to kiss her, to make love to her.

And—Brian Cutler pulled back.

Cherie got mad. Wasn't this guy human? Did he think she had the bubonic plague? She was throwing herself at him shamelessly. And he had the nerve to refuse what she was offering, to yank himself from her as though telling her he wanted to have nothing more to do with her.

Somebody once said that hell has no fury like that of a woman scorned. Cherie knew an anger that made her tremble. She opened her mouth to scream at him, but she also looked into his eyes—and read a deep misery in them.

"Something wrong?" she asked softly.

He nodded glumly. "It isn't right, what I was going to do. I'm sorry."

She gritted her teeth. "Oh? What was it you were about to do?"

"I shouldn't even talk about it."

"Go ahead. Talk about it."

"I have no right to hold you like this. Can't you understand that? I'm your lawyer, not your lover. Sure, sure, I love you. I can't deny that. But—"

"What did you say?" she asked weakly.

Brian blinked at her. "Haven't you been listening?"

I'll say I've been listening. But just repeat it, please!

Cherie nodded. "Oh, yes. I've been paying attention. But I'm not quite certain about that last part."

His smile was tender. "You mean when I said I loved you? Can't you tell how much I do? Idiot! I adore you. I

think you're the most beautiful woman God ever made.
But does it do me any good? It does not."

She swallowed, not quite certain that she was following
all this. If he loved her, why didn't he just pick her up and
carry her inside the cottage? He could prove how much he
loved her then, and she could certainly convince him that
he was the only man for her.

Cherie made herself say, "Good. You love me. I love
you. What are we waiting for?"

"I can't. You're an heiress. I'm your lawyer. It isn't eth-
ical."

Oh, my God! What does a girl do with a guy like this?

"I still don't understand. Maybe I'm dumb."

"There is such a thing as a lawyer-client relationship.
I'm not at liberty to fall in love with you—not when you
stand to inherit such a huge fortune. I don't want anybody
saying I fell in love with you because you're wealthy."

It was hard, but Cherie kept her temper. She mustn't
tell him what she was dying to yell at him. She must be
calm about this, just as easygoing as she could, under the
circumstances.

"I'm not wealthy yet. I don't have as much as fifty dollars to my name."

His smile was gentle. Cherie wished he would smile
more often like that because that smile did things to her,
deep inside.

"Not yet. But very soon. Think of it, Cherie. A billion
and a half dollars. Oak Haven as a home. Oil, ships,
banks. You'll own them all." He drew a deep breath.
"You know what the world will say about me if I do what
I want to do, with you?"

Who the hell cares about the world? This is between
you and me.

Morosely he went on. "The world will call me a fortune-hunter. A thief. An opportunist. Someone who took
advantage of an innocent girl to get hold of a huge fortune. I couldn't stand that."

Cherie sighed. The guy was a nut, all right. But deep inside her she understood that he was also being very honest.
Too damn honest, as a matter of fact. There wasn't anything she could do—or was there?

She tilted her head and looked up at him. She supposed
that all through the centuries, other women had had this
problem. Well, she didn't know about how other women

handled such things, but she knew very well what she was going to do.

"Sure, Brian," she heard herself say. "I understand. It's very noble of you, and I appreciate it."

His eyes widened. "You do? You're sure?"

She hugged him. "Certainly I'm sure. I think I'm very lucky to have found you as a lawyer. Now I don't have to worry about losing my money. I know that you'll do all you can to make certain I get it, and then take good care of it for me. I'm a very lucky girl."

He looked relieved. "I'm glad to hear you say that, Cherie. I've been worried lately, feeling as I do about you. I'm lucky to have you as a client."

Cherie smiled up at him. You don't know how lucky yet!

Aloud. she said, "You know what I'd like to do? Go for a swim. How about it?"

"That's a great idea. I know just the spot. No danger from water moccasins or alligators."

Cherie shivered, eyes wide. "Water moccasins? Alligators?"

"Well, sure. They abound in the bayou waters. But don't worry. Joe and I found a natural little basin where it's perfectly safe to swim. Give me a chance to fix us a sandwich and get into my trunks and I'll row us out there."

She wandered down to the water and stared at the pirogue. So he loved her but refused to touch her because she was an heiress, hey? Ha! There were ways to make a guy change his mind. He might play hard-to-get, but she was not going to give up all that easily. No way.

As he approached, she turned and gave him a smile. He was big and strong, his body was powerful. He would make a good lover. Even better, he would make a great husband. Cherie scowled. He would never marry her as long as she was an heiress, though. Unless, of course, she made herself so indispensable to him that he couldn't refuse to slip a wedding band around her finger.

So then. All she had to do was convince him.

Brian rowed the pirogue out into the bayou. Cherie let her gaze drift out across the water. The sun was warm, almost hot. It felt good on her skin. By the time they were ready to go swimming, she would be ready for a dip.

In time, he brought the pirogue to a narrow stretch of

marsh grass. Across it she could see what seemed to be a small lake set like a jewel in the greenery, with the moss-hung oaks girdling it. Brian rested on the oars as the pirogue moved slowly to the shore.

"That's where Joe and I used to swim long ago. No alligators are around, and we've never seen a water moccasin. But you'll have to be careful. Don't put your feet down too often. I'll be with you. You'll be all right."

Cherie nodded, let him help her from the pirogue. Might as well be helpless, she decided. Let him think she was absolutely unable to take care of herself, build up his male ego. As she moved through the marsh grass with him, she thought how wonderful it would be, being married to him and on their honeymoon, coming here day after day, without a worry in the world.

She dived in, seeing Brian dive with her, and swam beside him through the cool water. Her laughter rang out, to be echoed by his own. The sky was blue and cloudless above, the sun beat down on them. They were a primeval woman and man reveling in their health, in the delight of cool water on sun-warmed flesh. There was no one within miles, it was like a world all their own.

Brian was beside her, treading water, when she tired. She reached out to him, came closer until she was plastered up against him. "Hold me," she breathed. "I'm a little tired."

She wasn't tired at all, but it made a good excuse to have him put his arm around her, to lean against him this way, letting him know that he had a woman in his grasp. Her eyes smiled up at him, and she saw a tiny cloud of worry touch his eyes.

Ha! He wasn't so sure of himself right about now. Not with her flesh against his own, not with her arm about his neck and his arm about her bare middle. He might have a will of iron, but even iron melted, given the right conditions.

"It's perfect," she breathed. Cherie glanced up at the moss-hung trees, the sky. "It's ours, Brian—all ours."

"We'd better swim back," he said.

"Oh, not yet. Let's just enjoy the moment."

He was uneasy, she knew. It was all very well to tell her—from a distance—that she was a rich girl, that he really shouldn't have anything to do with her, even though he loved her, but up this close, in this bayou sanctuary, he was just talking. Maybe to keep himself from acting.

She wriggled against him, turning this way and that as though to observe the marsh grass and huge oaks that surrounded them. As she wriggled, she brushed against his body. Her face she ironed out to a childlike innocence, and she would not meet his eyes.

Her every movement was a caress. He could not help but be affected.

His hands came down on her hips.

Here it comes, he's going to push me away.

Instead, she felt those hands caressing her. Cherie leaned her face a little closer to his, turning to smile up into his eyes.

She caught her breath, vaguely alarmed at the raw hunger she could read in those eyes. "Brian—"

His arms drew her in against him. His lips descended on hers. Her mouth gave way slightly, opened. His arms were crushing her, driving the air from her lungs. But she was too excited to notice things like that. This was what she wanted, this was Heaven in capital letters and—

They went under, then came up, spluttering.

Brian said, "Sorry! I lost control. Come on, let's swim back to land."

Oooooh! He *would* have to kiss her here in the water. What she had to do now was get him to kiss her on dry land, perferably in the cottage. Cherie smiled to herself as she swam beside him. It shouldn't be too difficult. He was like a pile of sawdust, just awaiting the touch of flame to blaze up. She was the flame. And she was in control.

All that remained was to pick the time and place. Well, the time, anyhow. She knew the place, all right.

Brian was very quiet on the row back. He would not look at her, she noted; well, not very much, anyhow. But from time to time, she detected his eyes studying her, going over her body. And she also noted the deep hunger in them, the muted worship.

Cherie was very contented, sitting in the pirogue. It was so pleasant to sit here and plan her evening. It was late afternoon now. She felt very refreshed, her skin was cool, the sunlight felt good on her flesh. They would have their evening meal out in the yard and sit there until the stars came out.

After that—well, she had an idea of what it was she would do.

She helped Brian put the pirogue into the boat landing, then walked with him to the cottage. "I'm going to take a nice shower," she murmured. "Then I'll cook dinner. What would you like to eat?"

"Anything will do."

She moved ahead of him up the grassy slope and toward the cottage. She had to be very careful about this evening, she didn't want to scare this guy. As she thought this, she sneered. It should be the other way around, shouldn't it, with the man preparing for the big seduction scene, worrying about scaring *her?* Then her sense of humor came to the rescue.

The shower was delightful, she washed away everything but her body with the warm water, then tried a little cold water to tone her up. She tingled as she stepped out and dried herself. First came her perfume, then the little outfit she had decided on.

She had never worn the shorts and halter before, with Brian. She had almost forgotten about that outfit. First of all, it was so old! Threadbare, too. She wondered if she would fit into it. It was white, it would show off her tan admirably. As she drew it from a drawer, Cherie made a face. It really was rather skimpy, just as bad as her swimsuit.

Always, she had donned this thing to relax in at her apartment, nights when it was stifling in New Orleans, when she could be by herself and not care about how exposed she might be. Sighing, she wriggled into the short pants, then slid the bandeau about her. Hmmm. She still fit into it, but just about.

The mirror confirmed her worst fears. Why, this thing was positively indecent. Ha! It was just what she wanted. She giggled, turning to admire herself in the glass. It sure showed how she was constructed, all right. It left very little to the imagination.

"Good," she muttered. "This ought to open his eyes."

Cherie pattered out into the kitchen, began to remove hamburger patties from the fridge. Hamburgers and coffee. It might not be very romantic, but she would furnish the romance. Besides, she didn't want him concentrating so much on food that he would be able to ignore her.

She made a pot of coffee, put it on the burner. Then she

ran outside to start the charcoal fire. It was fun cooking for Brian. She just wished she had it to do all her life. She thought about that, watching the coals begin to glow. As a rich woman, she guessed she would have servants to cook for her, to bring her clothes, to do just about everything that she needed.

Cherie frowned. She didn't enjoy being waited on all that much. She thought about somebody else cooking Brian's meals, and scowled. "I suppose I can get used to it," she murmured.

What was keeping Brian? He wasn't hiding from her, was he? Did he guess at what she was planning for this evening? No, he couldn't. She had given him no hint, none at all.

Then she saw him, stepping from the cottage doorway with a cocktail shaker in his hand, together with two glasses.

"I thought we might have a—"

He came to a dead stop, staring. The cocktail shaker in his hand started to quiver. Brian cleared his throat. His eyes, Cherie saw with delight, ran over her again and again.

"You made cocktails," she exclaimed in a pleased voice. "That's wonderful. I think I could do with a drink."

"So could I." Brian nodded.

She walked toward him, reached out to take the glasses. Brian drew a deep breath and tilted the shaker to pour the martinis. His hands still shook a little, Cherie noted with glee.

Her hand raised her glass. "To us," she murmured.

Brian nodded solemnly. "To us."

They sipped, Cherie looking up into Brian's face while Brian stared out over the bayou waters.

"Oh, the hamburgers," she cried, and moved toward the grill. She was aware that Brian had removed his stare from the bayou and was now looking at her.

She turned her patties, then glanced back over her shoulder. "You'll have time for one more before we eat. Go ahead, but count me out."

Cherie wanted a clear head for the evening, but it wouldn't hurt if Brian was slightly whiffy. She wondered if two martinis would make him that way. Might be better if he had three. "Go on," she urged. "We have time."

She turned her head away so that he would not see her

little, secret smile. Drink, Brian. It will make you less tense. Of course, she did not want him to get drunk. That would be the ruination of her plans.

They ate side by side on the bench, with Cherie leaning against his shoulder, after a time. They sipped their coffee as the sun sank and the first stars came into the night sky.

"So peaceful here, so heavenly," she whispered.

He had put his arm about her by this time. She laid her head on his shoulder. She tilted her chin so that her mouth was only inches fom his own. He was looking up at the sky. Probably scared to look at me!

"They're so bright tonight, the stars," she murmured.

"Mmmm, yes."

"Almost as though you can reach out and catch hold of them."

It wasn't stars she wished he would reach out and catch hold of, but her. What was the matter with the guy? Here she had concocted those delicious hamburgers, the savory coffee, and all he could do was stare up at the sky. With a couple of martinis in him yet.

"You know what I'd like to do?" she asked.

"What?"

"I'd love to dance. Do you think we could? In the house, of course."

He hesitated. "Well, we do have a couple of radios. ..."

"Come on, then." She caught hold of his hand, drew him with her at a half-run toward the cottage. Her heart was singing as she moved, she was filled with love toward this man who ran with her.

She understood him now. He was afraid of being thought a fortune-hunter if he made a play for her. Well, the hell with that! He was the one man she wanted, and he could have all the scruples in the world. She was going to get him. She felt like a huntress, and had to smother a giggle.

Brian turned on the radio and fiddled with the dials while she switched on a soft light and kicked back the carpet. The floor was evenly laid, it would make a perfect dance floor. She glanced at Brian, bent above the radio, still fussing with the dials. Maybe he was hoping she would change her mind.

No way, buster.

As he straightened, she moved in on him, arms raised so that he had to put his arms about her. This brought her in close to him. Not as close as she wanted, though, so she wriggled somewhat nearer until she was just about plastered up against him.

They danced. Brian was a good dancer, he moved easily and in time to the music. For a little while she gave herself over to the music and rhythm, head resting on his upper chest. His hand was on her bare back, warm and comforting. It was so pleasant, this dancing close together, so dreamy. In a way, it was too bad they had to stop. But there would be a lot of other times to dance, Cherie reminded herself with a wicked little smile.

Right now, though . . .

His palm was moving against her back, as though caressing her. That hand sent shivers throughout her flesh. Was Brian feeling the same way as she was? But of course he was. She would not be a woman if she could not tell. His breathing was coming faster, his arm about her was tightening. His step faltered now and then. He sure wasn't thinking too much about dancing.

Well, neither was she, to tell the truth.

She looked up at him in the dim light. "You dance beautifully, Brian," she whispered.

"It's you. You're easy to dance with."

"Am I, Brian?"

His eyes were boring into hers. His arm was gathering her in, squeezing her. "I don't think we should be doing this," he murmured.

"Why not? Aren't you enjoying it?"

"Too much."

They were hardly moving now, just swaying slightly. He put his other arm about her, holding her rather firmly. In a moment he was going to kiss her. His arms tightened, drawing her so close that he could feel just about every curve of her front. As she could feel him, naturally.

His lips caught hers, held them. They strained together, Cherie lifting upward. Her senses began to swirl, faster and faster, and she started to lose control over every emotion she possessed. She was breathing faster—just as fast as he was, as a matter of fact.

Cherie knew vaguely that she had never felt like this, ever before. Her body was bursting, it grew harder to breathe, she seemed to be floating away in a golden cloud. His tongue touched hers, and she found herself sobbing and writhing against him.

"This is wrong," he whispered against her soft, moist mouth.

"Mmmmm," she moaned.

"I can't help myself," he groaned.

"Mmmm. Me neither."

"I'm losing my mind."

His arms went away, to slide under her and lift her high on his chest. His eyes blazed into hers. He was walking, she knew vaguely, carrying her somewhere. Her arms were locked about his neck; she discovered that she was kissing his chin, his cheek, his throat.

Then he was putting her down on a bed and sinking beside her, touching her, and her bandeau was falling away and her breasts were free and then his mouth was covering them, kissing, and Cherie was moaning steadily, hands buried in his hair.

"Forgive me," he was whispering excitedly. "I can't help myself."

She didn't even bother to answer that, she was so busy helping him get his own clothes off and then sliding out of those short-shorts she had on. There was bright moonlight flooding through the bedroom window, highlighting the bed, making everything almost as clear as sunlight.

He drew her against him, hugging her, holding her, whispering into her ear. "I adore you, Cherie. God forgive me, but I love you. I love you! I can't help myself. It's as though something stronger than I am has hold of me."

His hands were stroking her, caressing her. They moved here and there, and in answer to their touch, something deep within her was exploding again and again, until she wailed and wept, but with infinite delight. Her own hands were stretched out to him, exploring and stroking, and once she bit him on the shoulder, shuddering with the pleasure that ran all through her.

Neither of them spoke again. Their every sense was caught up in this explosion of pleasure. They clung and kissed, their hands went wild, and then, slowly, eyes closed, Cherie sank down upon her back.

Brian loomed above her, and her arms clasped him, held.

She cried out once, thickly, as pleasure ran riot in her flesh.

The night went on, and this delight was unending. . . .

12

Cherie woke slowly, filled with lassitude and a strange, muffled pleasure. Vaguely she was aware that there was a warm body close to her own, snuggled up tight to her. Something held her firmly, yet gently, too. For a long moment she lay with her eyes closed, enjoying this instant out of time.

Then her eyes snapped open.

She was in bed with Brian! Yes! It was Brian who held her so comfortingly, so warmly. Memory came flooding in on her and her lips curved in a lazy, contented smile.

I never imagined, even in my craziest dreams, that I could be so happy! And I owe it all to him!

She must not move. If she did, she might scare him away. And she wanted this moment to go on and on.

Still! Maybe she could be even happier. She began to turn, slowly and gently, so as not to awaken him. She managed it; he was still asleep, she saw as she swung about to face him.

How like a little boy he looked, with a lock of his black hair falling down over his forehead. His lips were smooth, gentle. Not fiercely passionate as they had been last night. Her fingertip touched his jaw, ran along it. He needed a shave, but what did that matter? He was hers now. All hers. Nobody else was ever going to get him. He was all hers.

She leaned to kiss him gently, and he opened his eyes.

At first those eyes reflected the love she felt. He was gazing at her in such tenderness, such love, that she had to swallow to keep from weeping. This was as it should be between them.

"Good morning," she whispered.

"Good morning."

Then his eyes widened and he would have started back

away from her except that Cherie had put both arms about his neck.

Brian moaned, "Forgive me," he mumbled. "I lost my head last night."

"What's to forgive? We love each other, don't we?"

Indignantly he muttered, "Of course we love each other, but what's that got to do with it? You're my client!" He sought to get away from her, but she clung to him relentlessly.

"I'm the woman you love," Cherie said softly. "This is perfectly right and natural. Now will you stop whipping yourself with words? Just relax and enjoy our being together."

He shook his head, but his lips smiled ruefully. "You aren't making this easy for me. Can't you see my position? I brought you here to protect you, and here I go, making love to you."

"Pooh! I wanted you to."

He had sunk back upon the bed, his arms had gone around her even as her arms were around him. Cherie smoothed back his tumbled hair, smiling up at him. His hands slid up and down her back, making her shiver.

"I wanted to, myself." He chuckled with a wry grin. "But that doesn't excuse me. I've violated a trust."

Cherie scowled playfully. "You keep arguing so much I get the feeling that you're sorry you did it."

He was stricken. "Never that! You just don't understand."

"If you're worried about the fact that I may inherit so much money, forget it. I don't want it."

"You can't refuse it!"

"I can if it means I won't be happy," she yelled, her temper beginning to get the better of her. Then she calmed and moved closer, whispering, "I'll be happy only with you."

He stared down into her eyes tenderly, whispering, "I know what I ought to do, but I can't." He kissed her, gently at first, then hungrily. He paused to murmur, "I ought to tear myself away from you and go back to New Orleans and leave you here." He kissed her again, then whispered, "But I can't. All I want is you."

"Well, then—"

His kiss smothered her words, and she felt herself caught up and gripped in a maelstrom of pleasure. It was as though the entire world went away somewhere and left them here alone on this bed, toying with each other, rousing each other to the very peak of bliss, of happiness.

Cherie floated off somewhere, adored and worshiped; she wanted this to go on and on, and never stop. Pleasure and delight so intense she cried out and wept, ran through her. She arched and shuddered, her soft cries of enjoyment echoing in the room. It went on and on. . . .

Much later, she opened her eyes, to find Brian nestled close beside her, staring down into her face. She smiled and blew a kiss at him.

"I wish," he began, and then shook his head.

"What?" she asked dreamily. "What do you wish?"

"I wish I could take you somewhere and marry you. I wish I could make you my wife for the rest of my life."

Cherie giggled. "That's what a girl likes to hear. Now why can't you?"

"Because you're a Mannering. You're going to inherit a billion and a half dollars, and you're going to move in a completely different circle than I am."

"Not me. All I want is you."

Brian sighed. "Let's go have breakfast."

She had to do something to convince him that he could marry her even if she was a wealthy woman, Cherie decided. Why couldn't the guy be a fortune-hunter? What was so wrong with that? Ha! She probably wouldn't love him if he were. Life gets mighty complicated sometimes, she reflected wryly.

She lay there and watched as he moved from the bed. He had a good body, she noted. Muscles rippled all over it. No wonder he could squeeze her so tightly! It was a body she wanted, forever. Cherie smiled to herself. Getting it was up to her. She had to find a way to do away with those crazy ideas of his about being a fortune-hunter. Once she did that, it would be clear sailing.

She drowsed, eyelids closed. She could hear Brian moving about in the kitchen, and she knew that she would have to get up very soon. What would she do today? What she would like to do is have Brian come back here and make love to her all day long. But he would never agree to that! Hmmmm. Yesterday she had started that self-portrait. She would work on it today, maybe even finish it.

She would make Brian a present of it. A sort of love offering. Yes, that was what she would do! She slid out of bed, ran for the shower. She dressed quickly in her sun-suit, telling herself that no matter how many clothes she ever bought in the future, she would always keep that sun-suit.

They ate breakfast side by side, pausing from time to time to kiss. There seemed to be no reluctance now in Brian to kissing her. Maybe he realized he had made his fight and lost.

Once as they were kissing, Cherie whispered against his lips, "You have to go away today, somewhere."

He drew back. "Oh? Why is that?"

"I want to finish that painting, and I never will with you around. All I really want to do is hang on to you and keep kissing you and making love. But," she added with a sigh, "I'll never finish that picture if I do."

"All right. I'll go out clamming. We could stand a feast of clams."

For long hours Cherie labored over her self-portrait. Yesterday she had had trouble with it; it had not seemed to come out the way she wanted it, but today she seemed to have an affinity with the oils and the canvas, or they with her, because as the afternoon shadows lengthened, she stood back to study it and was pleased. She had captured just the expression she wanted.

Would Brian like it? He had to! If he didn't enthuse over it, she knew she would be horribly disappointed. But why shouldn't he like it? It was she, Cherie Marsan, with a pleasant smile on her lips, a smile she had managed to capture in the eyes as well.

Cherie paced back and forth, staring at the bayou, wondering what was keeping him. He probably was giving her all the time she needed to do a good job. After all, she had been the one who had sent him away, with instructions to stay as long as possible. Occasionally she would wander back to her painting and stare at it, wondering if it were the best she could do. She was half-tempted to begin all over again, but something inside her told her to be satisfied.

Shadows were lengthening along the ground when Brian came back to the boathouse with two buckets filled with clams and some fish on a string. Cherie moved to meet him, oddly shy about letting him see what she had done.

He kissed her gently, then walked with his arm about

her middle toward the easel. He halted a dozen feet away and stared. Then he turned to look into her face.

"You've captured it," he said with intense satisfaction.

Cherie stared at him.

"Your resemblance to Lavinia. Can't you see it?"

She looked more closely at her portrait. Well, now that he had pointed it out again, she saw what he meant. Hmmm! She did look a lot like that ancestress of hers. Yet she had painted herself as the little mirror told her she looked like. It was something she had done almost instinctively. She had forgotten Lavinia Mannering while she had been working.

"Now that you mention it"—she nodded—"I see what you mean. Hey, this won't do."

"It certainly will! It's perfect."

Cherie frowned. "But I don't look that much like her, do I? Really?"

"You could be her twin. It's perfect. Just what I want." Brian rubbed his hands together in deep satisfaction.

"But—"

"Hey! I'm going to take this to those estate lawyers and let them compare it to that painting of Lavinia Mannering. If that doesn't convince them, nothing will."

Cherie pursed her lips. "I painted it for *you.*"

He grabbed her, kissed her. "And I'm grateful. I'm going to hang it up in my room back at River View. But it's going on loan for a time, to the lawyers. I want them to have it in their hands when they take it to Oak Haven and compare it to that oil painting of Lavinia. Come on, let's go get dinner ready. I'm starved."

As she walked with him toward the cottage, Cherie told herself that she was hungry also. She had forgotten all about lunch, what with concentrating so much on her painting.

"A feast of clams and fish. "I'll get busy and open the clams. You set up the coals."

She nodded, wondering why she felt a little let down. Of course! She had done the picture for him, for the man she loved. And here he was, talking about giving it to those lawyers. Well, not giving it exactly, but loaning it to them. Her better judgment told her he was doing it for her, to help her get that billion-odd inheritance. She ought to be glad.

Yet a little resentment lingered. Oh, he had enthused

over it, sure. But what he should have done was catch her up in his arms and smother her with kisses.

Ha! Maybe he had spent the whole day arguing with himself. Telling himself that she was going to be a rich woman very soon and that she would have no time for the likes of him. Cherie gritted her teeth. What did she have to do to make this guy understand that she didn't care about any inheritance, that all she wanted was Brian Cutler?

She slid her eyes sideways at him. He could not be so indifferent toward her. Certainly—not after last night! As a woman, she knew better. But with a guy like Brian Cutler, with all those high ideals of his, maybe he would change his mind.

"I'll go shower," she murmured.

"Sure. Go ahead."

He could have delayed her for a hug and a kiss, she told herself as she moved into her room. It was almost as though nothing at all had happened between them. He had gone back into his shell, and she seemed to know that it would take some prying to get him out of it. As she took her shower, it seemed to her that she might be crying a little, but if she was, the warm water was washing away her tears.

Brian had opened the clams by the time she emerged in skirt and sweater. No more sunsuit. If he didn't want her, it wouldn't help her to go around almost stark naked. She moved past him without saying a word, going out to dump charcoal briquettes into the grill. She poured liquid on the briquettes and touched a match to them, then stood and stared down into the flames.

This morning she had been so happy. Now she was miserable. Maybe that was what love was like. Cherie didn't know, she had never been in love before. But right now she wished with all her heart that Brian would come up behind her, grab her, and kiss her.

Then he was beside her, with the fish he had cleaned and scaled on two big platters. His smile was friendly as he said, "Just as soon as those coals get hot, we'll put the fish on. I've opened the clams and prepared the sauce. Would you like to eat out here, the way we did last night?"

I certainly would! Then after we eat we can go back into the bedroom and make love.

Cherie said, "I guess so. I'll set the places."

They ate the clams while the fish cooked, and drank wine, enjoying the stillness of this corner of the bayou. It was a calm time of day, this early evening, with the sun setting and casting longer and longer shadows. From time to time Cherie glanced at Brian, discovering that he was frowning in thoughtful concentration.

When would he suggest they go to bed?

Then he said, "Tomorrow I have to get up early. I'm going into New Orleans."

Cherie stared. "Do you think it's safe?"

He chuckled. "You're going to stay here. I'm going alone."

"But why? Why are you leaving me?"

It seemed to Cherie that her heart had stopped. To be left alone in this wilderness, all by herself? What would happen to her?

"To make sure you get what should be yours. Now that you've done that painting, I can take it to the estate lawyers, get them to check it with the painting of Lavinia Mannering so that they can see the close resemblance. It ought to be the clincher."

"Brian, I don't care about the estate. Just stay with me. Please?"

He swung around, caught her hands, held them tightly as he stared deep into her eyes. "Cherie, I'm doing this for you. You don't realize yet what it's like to have all that money and power. It means you can go anywhere you want, not only in comfort but in luxury. You can have anything you want, anything at all!"

Even—you? Will it give me you, all that money? I'm getting the feeling that it won't, that you're too stubborn, too high-minded, to marry me, when I'll be that rich!

Aloud, she muttered, "I'd rather have you stay here."

"And I'd rather stay, believe me. But my first duty is as your attorney, to get you everything that belongs to you. That's why I have to get back to the city, to see those lawyers."

There was no sense in arguing with him when he got that stubborn look on his face. No words from her would sway him. She doubted very much whether anything she did would tempt him from what he conceived to be the right thing. Cherie gritted her teeth, wishing he wasn't so high-minded.

"You'd leave me all alone?"

His face mirrored his surprise as he turned to her. "You'll be perfectly safe. No one will bother you. Believe me, Cherie."

There was nothing she could do to change his mind, she knew. Especially when he said, "We'd better get a good night's sleep. I want to be in tip-top shape tomorrow, in case those estate lawyers give me a lot of flak."

Cherie nodded, but she sensed that he was just saying that to get out of making love to her. He probably figured if he did it again, he wouldn't be able to leave her. And he had to leave her to get that picture to Regan, Hennessey, and LeBlanc. She wished she had never painted the damn thing.

He was gone the next morning when she woke and went out into the kitchen. She had peeped into his bedroom—he had slept alone last night, of course—and when she saw the car gone, she knew he had chickened out. He hadn't dared to stay and say good-bye to her. Cherie sneered as she heated the coffee.

The day stretched before her. She wandered from room to room in the cottage, looking for something to do. She made her bed—he had already made his, after a fashion—and then sat down and looked out a window. Tiring of that, she walked outside, to wander up and down the grass, eyeing the bayou waters, the distant trees.

After a time she went down to the pirogue, got out the oars, and rowed out into the bayou. She rowed until she was weary, telling herself that she would sleep better at night if she were exhausted. When she came in sight of the little lake where they had gone swimming, she urged the boat toward shore.

She didn't have a swimsuit, so she took off her clothes and plunged into the water. She swam vigorously, enjoying the coolness of the water, but it wasn't the same without Brian beside her. To dry off, she lay down on the grass for an hour, turning over from time to time.

As she rowed back to the cottage, tears welled up in her eyes. She should be the happiest girl in the world, but she wasn't. She was going to inherit more than a billion dollars, if all went well and she really was Josiah Mannering's granddaughter. One could do a lot with that much money. Ha! She would gladly have traded all of it in for a wedding ring from Brian Cutler.

Brian Cutler was not about to slip a wedding ring on her finger, though. Not if she became a billionairess. Hey! Maybe he would fail. Maybe she wasn't Clarissa Theresa Mannering, after all. So she looked like that old picture, like Lavinia Mannering. Big deal! She was just her double, that's all.

Cherie felt a little better as she eased the pirogue in under the landing shed. Brian had no real *proof*. A likeness and a story about some woman who had taken refuge with the Marsans. That was all it amounted to. Supposition, pure and simple.

She tied the rope that held the pirogue and straightened up. Sure. He would lose his claim for her, she would be left without a cent. She would be just a penniless artist again. No more, no less.

Cherie grinned. "Then he won't have any excuse, by golly. Then he'll marry me." Her face clouded. "Won't he? He hasn't been just stringing me along, has he?"

No, she knew better than that. It was she who had practically forced him into bed with her, not the other way around. Brian had been very circumspect. He really believed that she was Clarissa Mannering. She grinned wryly. What a situation! Either she had to take a billion and a half dollars and lose the man she loved, or give up all that dough and be able to marry Brian.

She kicked the turf as she walked along. What was money without him? Brian was all she asked out of life. She would gladly have traded all that property and cash in order to get him.

Cherie came to an abrupt stop, staring.

There was a car in the driveway, a sleek Continental. Cherie's brows almost met in a dark scowl. She knew that car, all right! It belonged to that redheaded woman who kissed Brian whenever she saw him. Cara Slagle. Her eyes roamed across the grass. She wasn't in sight.

Hey! She must be in the cottage. The cottage that Cherie considered to be hers. Well, hers and Brian's, that is. Instantly she strode forward, her anger gathering slowly inside her.

As she was about to reach for the knob, the door swung open and Cara Slagle stood there, looking down her nose at her. Cherie swallowed. She had to admit, this was one beautiful woman! Her silk jacket, that flared skirt she was wearing, the blouse showing slightly beneath the jacket, the jewels on her fingers . . .

"Where is he?" Cara asked coldly.

"None of your business," Cherie snapped.

Cara Slagle smiled down at her, chillingly sweet. "Isn't it, my good woman? Isn't it, indeed? Now you listen to me. Sure, I know you've been playing around with Brian, but he's a man and I suppose he has to get something out of his system. That's why he picked up with someone like you."

The anger in her swirled upward, almost blinding her. Cherie had to grab hold of herself with all her willpower to prevent her from hurling herself at this stuck-up bitch and pounding on her with her fists. For the first time she actually wanted to be proven Clarissa Mannering, just so she could flaunt her millions in this one's face!

"He's with me because he hopes to earn a big legal fee," she found herself saying.

Incredulity showed in Cara's brown eyes. "A legal fee? From such as *you*? Don't make me laugh!"

"Laugh all you want. It's true."

For the first time Cara Slagle seemed to draw back and look at her more closely. Those brown eyes ranged all over her, taking her in from the top of her yellow hair to the soles of her worn sneakers. Doubt and bafflement warred for an instant in those eyes.

What sort of case could *you* have?"

Cherie grinned up at her. "One that's interesting Brian enough to have him drop every other case he has and concentrate on mine."

Ah, that stung the redhead. Cherie saw that, knew it deep in her heart. The doubt in Cara's eyes changed to wonderment. Then she gestured with a hand. "I don't believe it," she snapped.

"Who cares what you believe?" She considered the other woman from under her long golden lashes. "But you have to admit that Brian ran off here into bayou country with me. And not for any purpose you might be thinking about, either. Not just because I'm a woman and he's a man. Rather because I have a very important claim and he's my lawyer.

"Tell me," she added, "from what you know of Brian, do you think he'd come away out here and leave his law practice just because he might want a roll in bed with me?"

The doubt in Cara Slagle's face became grim certainty. "No," she admitted honestly. "Brian isn't like that. It's always duty above everything else with him."

She looked at Cherie with new eyes. Suddenly she turned and widened the door, extending a hand invitingly. "Come on in. Let's have a little talk, you and I. Oh, by the way—where's Brian?"

Cherie grinned triumphantly. "He went into New Orleans with a picture of me. He tells me that picture is going to make me wealthy."

To her surprise, Cara Slagle began to laugh.

13

Cherie stepped past her and walked into the cottage, resisting the urge to wipe that laugh off her face by scratching it. Never in her life had she so disliked anyone as she disliked Cara Slagle. It was only by an effort of will that she fought back that urge to belt her one.

Cara followed her, closing the door behind her. "So then, you're an artist. You must be pretty good, though, if Brian is taking an interest in your work. I suppose he thinks you're a genius?"

The sarcasm just about dripped from her mouth. Cherie stiffened herself against it, willing a smile upon her lips. It was time to wipe that sneer and that laughter from this woman.

"I didn't say that. Oh, yes, I'm an artist, but not a very good one, I'm afraid. Certainly not good enough for Brian to drop everything and concentrate his legal skills on me."

There. That ought to knock the wind out of this rich bitch. Cherie reveled in the change of expression that slid across Cara Slagle's face. Haughtiness merged into doubt, and the doubt changed to confusion as the other woman eyed her.

"Then what is it? What made him bring you out here to this godforsaken spot and hide away with you?"

"I'm afraid it's a bit of a secret right now. Brian's working very hard on my case, that's why he left me to run into the city. He claims that picture I did will help him prove his case."

Cherie smiled sweetly, enjoying the puzzlement of the other girl. Cara appeared to draw herself up.

"Well? What is that case?"

"Can't tell you. Why don't you ask Brian?"

Cara nibbled at a lip. "Why is it such a secret?"

"Well, for one thing, men have been trying to kill me." She watched the shock register on Cara's face, then went

126

on. "Brian figured I'd be safe here from assassins. Does that answer all your questions?"

Cara Slagle nodded slowly. "In a way, yes. Brian would do something like this if your life were in danger. If anyone's life were in danger, for that matter—even a dog's." Her smile grew. "He's like that, a real romanticist. In that case, I suppose it's all right."

Her eyes swept over Cherie coldly. "However, I still don't like it. I want you to know that Brian is mine, do you understand? I don't want you trying to take him away from me, just because he's idiot enough to take you out here and hide you away from somebody. As far as that goes, if someone wants to kill you, maybe you deserve killing."

And you'd like to be the one to pull the trigger, too, wouldn't you?

Cara added, "Girls sometimes get into trouble over their heads. Then someone like Brian has to save them from the consequences of their acts."

"Oh, it isn't like that at all." Cherie laughed. Let the bitch simmer and stew in her bile! Let her try and find out why it was she was here with Brian. She certainly wasn't going to tell her any more than she already had.

The red eyebrows shot up. "Oh, no? Then what is it like?"

Cherie shook her head. "Sorry. I just can't tell you."

Cara paced up and down the rug. She was like a coiled spring, about to unwind and fly in all directions. Cherie watched her carefully. If she leaps at me, I'm going to belt her one, I really am! Apparently Cara saw this, for she came to an abrupt halt.

"I can find out all I want to know from Brian's brother. You understand that? It was he who told me where I could find Brian. I came out here with some legal papers for him to check—and I thought that while I was here, I might stay a few days with him."

"And a few nights too, perhaps? If I weren't here to spoil your plans!"

Cara smiled sweetly. "I *could* sleep with him."

"Over my dead body!"

Oops! She hadn't meant to let that come out. Oh, well. Cara might as well know now as later that she wasn't going to get Brian Cutler. No way.

Cara sneered. "No need for such dramatics." Her eyes

went over Cherie from top to bottom, assessed her, then dismissed her. "If you're his client, he certainly won't go to bed with you. He can with me, however."

"You're his client, too."

Cara shrugged. "I'm something more than a client to Brian."

Is that so? What would you say if I told you that Brian and I had already slept together?

"I wouldn't know about that. I guess a lawyer has to take whatever business comes his way," she said aloud, and delighted in the indignant look Cara Slagle threw at her.

Cara Slagle moved away then, picking up her pocket-book and driving gloves from an end table. She crossed the room to the door, halting there and turning to glance back at Cherie.

"I'll be back," she said ominously, "when Brian is here to talk to me." She paused, and added, "I'm not used to conducting my business with servant girls."

She opened the door and stepped out. Cherie took a step toward her, her hands balled into fists. She ran to the door and watched as Cara got into her car and started it, turned it, and drove off down the dirt road.

So much for that. Ha! As if she didn't have enough to worry her about Brian, without Cara Slagle looming up on the horizon. Miserably she told herself that if she didn't convince Brian he ought to marry her, Cara would surely get him. Her enjoyment of the day was gone.

She walked up and down the lawn, then wandered down to the boathouse, seating herself by the edge of the bayou waters. She felt lost, somehow. It was as though a part of her had died back there while she had been with Cara Slagle. But why should she feel that way?

Of course, ninny. Cara was from Brian's social crowd. She was his equal, she was used to the things Brian knew, she had shared them with him. Her home would be as grand as his, maybe even more luxurious. And what was she, Cherie Marsan? A nobody. Oh, sure, a pretty girl. But she was confident that Brian had known other girls just as pretty. What made her think she would be able to get him?

Certainly not because she might inherit more than a billion dollars! He had made that quite plain. And what do I have to offer him, except poor me? It isn't enough, Cherie

—and you know it! Tears came from her eyes and slid slowly down her cheeks. She wished she were dead. Then she wouldn't have all these problems to face.

She rubbed her eyes, got to her feet, and began walking toward the dirt road that ran through this part of the bayou country. She could make out the tire marks from the Continental. Cherie gritted her teeth. If she got that fortune, Brian would get Cara—or Cara would sink her fangs into Brian. She herself would be left out in the cold.

She walked on along the road, scuffing her feet. If she had the courage—and a car—she would drive out of here, go someplace else where nobody would ever find her. Then Brian would be sorry! Her lips twisted in a mock smile. Brian would forget her soon enough. Especially with Cara Slagle to help him.

She saw an old log, long since fallen off to one side of the road. Cherie went and sat on it, chin on her fist, staring into nothingness. It was time for lunch, she supposed, but she was not hungry. She might never eat again. Why should she eat? It would only keep her alive. Phooey! Who wanted to be alive and as miserable as she was? She would be better-off if she were dead.

How long she sat there, staring into the forest, she would never know. Only when she heard a sound did she rouse up out of her lethargy to listen. That was a car motor she heard. Was Cara Slagle coming back? She rose to her feet, staring down the length of the dirt road.

She saw a glint of sunlight on metal, then the car was coming around a bend and heading toward her. Her heart almost stopped beating. It was Brian! He had finished with his business in New Orleans and had come back to her. She raised her arms and waved them, yelling.

He braked at sight of her and she ran to him, yelling, "You came back. You came back."

Brian laughed. "Certainly I came back, silly. Did you think I was going to leave you all alone here? Here, get in and drive back with me."

He opened the door and she scrambled in, squirming across the seat so as to be closer to him. His eyes went all over her face and Cherie realized with dismay that her eyes and cheeks might reveal that she had been crying. Well, she had. And so what? She had missed him!

"You all right?" he asked.

"Sure. What makes you think I'm not?"

"Just thought you might have missed me."

"Naturally I missed you. It was lonely there at the cottage without you. Until that bitch came."

"Let me guess now. That would have to be Cara Slagle. Right?"

She glowered at him. "It was Cara, putting on airs, telling me that she was going to get hooks in you no matter what I did."

Brian chuckled. "I doubt if she put it quite like that."

"Maybe not so bluntly, but you can bet that's what she had in mind."

He pulled the Granada up before the cottage and turned to her, shutting off the motor. "Aren't you at all interested in what I've been doing for you?"

Cherie shrugged. Sure, you've been trying to prove me out to be Clarissa Theresa Mannering, and so what? She stared straight ahead through the windshield.

"Those estate lawyers were quite taken by that picture you did of yourself. They've been doing some work on their own, too, I'm happy to say. Looking through a lot of books and papers in Oak Haven."

"So?"

"They came across a baby book with Clarissa Mannering's baby fingerprints in it."

He sat back and beamed at her. Cherie glanced at him from the corners of her eyes. "What's that got to do with me?"

"Those will prove to be your fingerprints. I'm willing to bet my life on it. There won't be any argument against those."

Cherie went on scowling. Why couldn't he forget all about the Mannering estate and just marry her? That was what she wanted. What he wanted, too, she felt sure. But, oh, no. Not him. He had to be the lawyer determined to make her a rich woman, no matter what she had to say about it.

"I'll inherit all that money, you mean?"

"You most certainly will."

"Then you'll be happy, won't you?" she flared. "You'll have done your job and made me wealthy and—and—"

She broke down then and bawled. She could not help it. The tears came out and flooded down her cheeks. She sobbed, she wailed. I want to die! I don't want to go on living any longer! She was vaguely aware of Brian's shocked incredulity, aware that he was reaching out and drawing her to him, folding his arms about her and holding her, whispering soothing words into her tumbled yellow hair just over her ear.

"Hey, hey. Take it easy. My God, I thought you'd be happy. I've been doing all this for you and now you seem to want to chuck the whole thing. Or is it that you're overwhelmed with happiness?"

"A lot you know." She sobbed.

His hand was smoothing her hair, even as he squeezed her. "Tell me, what is it? Did Cara say something to upset you?"

"Ha! That one!"

"Then what is it?"

She looked at him through tear-wet eyes. "Ca-can't you g-guess?"

He looked so stunned, so disconcerted, that she had to laugh through her tears. The idiot didn't have the slightest idea as to why she was so upset. Nor was she going to tell him. If he wasn't bright enough to figure it out for himself, she wouldn't help him.

"Look. I'm your lawyer. You can confide in me."

Ooooh! Her fists doubled up. She pounded on his shoulders. "Stupid! Stupid! Stupid! Just like a man! Why must you be so thick, so insensitive?"

His arms were drawing her toward him, crushing her hands and arms against his chest. Not only that, they were drawing her face closer to his own. Her eyes were so blurry with tears that she could not quite make out his expression, but next instant his lips were coming down on hers, mashing them.

"Mmmmmm," she murmured.

His arms tightened, his lips grew even hungrier. Cherie nestled against him, kissing him just as wildly as he was kissing her. A tiny corner of her mind whispered that maybe now he would understand what her trouble was. If only he would kiss her and hug her like this, instead of talking all the time!

He appeared to have caught her thoughts, because he went on kissing her wildly, crazily, as though he wanted to eat her up. She lay cuddled against him, trying to tell him to go on doing just what he was doing. Forget I'm an heiress! Forget all about the money I may be going to get!

Just love me, Brian. Love me! Cherie wanted to lie against him like this forever.

It had to stop, though. Even she knew that. Finally he drew back, staring down at her with wide eyes.

"What got into me?" he whispered. "Cherie, forgive me. I just lost control there."

Couldn't he ever kiss her without apologizing for it afterward? Cherie sighed. She muttered, "Will you stop saying you're sorry you kissed me? It doesn't do a girl any good to hear that."

His grin was lopsided. "Well, I'm not sorry. Not really, I guess. I certainly wanted to kiss you. Very badly. But a lawyer doesn't do these things."

"Why not? Isn't a lawyer human?"

"Sure he is. But there are duties he has, obligations that—"

"Brian, I'll hit you one."

He paused then and they stared at each other. He shook his head slowly. "All right. I'll level with you. I'm so nuts about you all I can think of is you. I love you, Cherie. I love you so much it hurts. But—"

Her hand covered his mouth as she smiled up at him. "No buts. Don't spoil it."

Brian shook his head, groaning. "I wish I could make you understand."

"There's only one thing I want to understand. You said you love me. Do you?"

"Well, of course I do! You're in my thoughts morning, noon, and night." He grinned. "Especially at night."

Cherie giggled. "Good. That's what I want to hear."

"You're a funny girl. Here you are, about to inherit over a billion dollars and all you seem to want is to have me make love to you."

"What's wrong with that?" she asked. Then: "No! Don't say a word. I'll tell you what you were going to say. 'Cherie, I love you, but you are my client and lawyers and clients don't go around kissing and hugging and making love.' Hey? Isn't that it?"

Brian laughed. "You have it down pat."

"Then phooey on it."

He drew back a little, frowning slightly. "You don't really mean that?"

"I most certainly do! Can't you forget you're a lawyer and I'm a client even for a little while? Couldn't you pretend you're just a guy and I'm a girl? That we're off here in the bayous for a little enjoyment out of life?"

"If I did . . ."

He halted, looking at her oddly. Cherie tilted up her chin at him. "If you did—what?"

"I'd scare you to death," he moaned.

"Oh, yeah?"

His arms grabbed her and yanked her against him. His mouth came down on hers and crushed her lips. Cherie felt whirled up and shaken until she didn't know which end was up. And she loved it! Her heart thumped and pounded, the blood ran through her gurgling and singing, and what difference did it make if she couldn't breathe?

The kissing and the hugging went on for quite a long time. Even Cherie had to admit that. But at last she lay there in his arms, with him kissing her throat, her cheeks, her eyelids, and told herself she was the happiest girl in the whole world. She wouldn't change places with anybody. Ha! Let them keep their billion and a half dollars. She knew what she wanted, all right. And it wasn't money.

She stirred finally, murmuring, "I suppose you're starved to death. You didn't eat any breakfast, either."

He whispered, "All I could think of was getting back to you. I missed you more than I can say."

"Try." She giggled.

His laughter was half muffled in her thick yellow hair. "Okay, I will. All the way into the city I kept kicking myself all over the car."

Her eyes widened. "Kicking yourself?"

"For having let you sleep alone. I ought to have dragged you into bed and made love to you until dawn."

She nodded vigorously. "You should have, Brian."

He laughed full-throatedly. "You know I can't believe this? Here I am holding you, kissing you, and I'm saying, 'To hell with my conscience!' What sort of lawyer am I turning out to be? My brother would be horrified."

"What's your brother got to do with it?"

"He's a stickler for doing the right thing all the time."

"Does he ever have any fun?"

"Joe? Hmmm. I never thought about it. I guess not. He works days and nights, he never even takes time off anymore."

"I don't want you to be like that."

He tilted her face upward with a finger under her chin.

His eyes glowed down at her. "When you're around, I don't want to be."

He kissed her then, very gently, very tenderly. The kiss went on and on, until Cherie decided it would be more comfortable in the cottage. After all, a car had never been designed for lovers.

"How would you like me to fix us something to eat?" she asked after a time.

"Only if I can help. You see, that way I can stay near you all the time."

"You can toast the bread."

"What will you be doing?"

"Oh, I'll think of something." She giggled.

"All right. Just stay there. I'll be around to help you out."

Then he was running around the car, opening the door and reaching in for her. She came into his arms easily, was lifted out, and set down on the ground. Brian put his arms around her and squeezed her into him. He began kissing her. Cherie had her arms about him, and was wholeheartedly entering into the spirit of the occasion, telling herself that this was the kind of lawyer for a girl to have.

When they finally broke apart, she tucked her arm in his and practically danced all the way beside him. Then she pushed him toward the bathroom, saying, "You go wash up. I'll start getting things ready for dinner."

Her heart was singing as she worked, her feet flew here and there, her hands were swift and deft while she set out a thick steak to be charcoal-broiled as she mixed salad. By the time Brian came to join her, she was almost finished.

"You didn't leave anything for me to do." He grinned.

"You're going to cook the steak. Set the fire. I'll make some cocktails and we'll have them outside while the coals are getting hot."

It was very pleasant, Cherie thought as she sat beside Brian, leaning against him and sipping her martini. The warmth of the day was fading into the coolness of early evening; it was good to smell the steak cooking, to taste the tartness of the cocktail, to know Brian's arm was around her, holding her. A girl couldn't ask for anything more.

Well, now. She could ask that this piece of heaven would go on and on, of course. That there would never be

an end to it. That Brian would see the light and marry
her, money or no money. She wondered for a moment if,
after she got all those millions of dollars, whether such a
wealthy woman would be able to run off somewhere like
this cottage and know such peace.

Still, why not? She could hire people to look after her
wealth, couldn't she? She'd bet all millionaires didn't sit
around watching over their interests all the time. Some of
them must take an interest in life, aside from the accumu-
lation of money. Ha! She would be one of those.

They ate side by side, completely content. Now that
Brian was filled with food and was sipping his second cup
of coffee, he was using his eyes on her, noting that her
shirt and slacks clung to her here and there. Cherie decided that she liked that glint in his eyes.

"We'd better get the dishes done," she said demurely.

"Let them go." He smiled, catching her by the hand.

Cherie raised her eyebrows. "Oh? In such a rush?"

He yanked her to her feet and in against him. "I've
been away from you for years. At least, it seemed like
years." He drew her even closer, wrapping his arms about
her.

Brian kissed her, and Cherie melted. She felt herself
being whirled off into a world where they were the only
living things, where this fire in each of them was exploding
outward, becoming one. Her own arms held him fiercely,
she urged her body to his.

Then she was being swept up and carried toward the
cottage, was aware that he was moving through the house
with her and into his bedroom. He let her go only to put
her on her feet and then he was undoing buttons, tugging
at her slacks belt to loosen it. Her own hands were just as
busy, she realized after a time, helping him.

They clung at the edge of the bed, whispering words
that had no meaning, saying things that made no sense,
yet seemed very appropriate at this moment. Cherie
tumbled backward—or was pushed—and Brian was there
on the bed with her, kissing her all over, and she was
whimpering, sighing, begging him to be with her forever
like this.

Pleasure exploded in her, and she wailed, knowing that
this was why she had been born, why she lived. This
madness was so ecstatic that she could not resist it even if
she had wanted. And so she gave herself up to it entirely,

crying out, experiencing an intensity of delight that lifted her out of the world and into a realm where nothing existed but this instant of madness, which went on and on. . . .

14

Something was tickling her ear. No, not tickling—blowing on it. Sleepily Cherie lifted a hand to brush away whatever it was. And something bit her fingers. Not hard, but very gently. Cherie opened her eyes wide.

She turned, saw Brian grinning down at her. "Wake up, angel. Time to be going."

He kissed her ear and Cherie made noises that indicated how nice it was to be waked in this manner. She put her arms around him and cuddled closer.

Brian was chuckling. "Much as I'd like to spend the day here with you, there are things we have to do."

"Eat later," she mumbled.

"New Orleans is waiting."

"Don't want New Orleans. Just want you."

"Sure. You have me. Now I have to give you all the rest of what you're going to get. Rise and shine, lovebird."

"Why? Isn't it nice and cozy in here, just you and me?"

He nibbled on her ear. Cherie thought that was very sweet of him to want to eat her ear. She wriggled against him happily.

"There's a fingerprint expert waiting, love of my life. We mustn't keep him waiting."

"Ohhh! You're always so—so down-to-earth."

"Just because I want to hand you heaven on a golden platter."

She grinned up at him. "I have heaven right here."

"Please?"

When he put it like that, Cherie could not refuse him. She sighed and nodded. "I suppose this is where it begins, all the problems I'm going to have with money. A rich girl can't sleep late, I suppose. She has to get up and—and sign papers and look at things and do whatever it is rich girls do."

"Right. And I'll be there to advise you."

As a lawyer or as a husband? Cherie wondered. Hmmm! If she had anything to do with it, and she did, it would be as her husband. She had never been as happy in her life as when she and Brian had been in bed together. Of course, she knew that was only one phase of married life, but the days she had spent here with Brian had convinced her that the other parts of being married—sharing meals, talking, and walking together—would be just as wonderful.

She leaned to kiss him, then sprang from the bed, racing toward the shower. She would have to wear her good clothes today, she was going to see that lawyer again, and she wanted to make a good showing for Brian's sake. She turned on the handles, adjusted the water, and stepped under it. She soaped and sang, and told herself that she was a very happy, lucky girl.

They ate breakfast in the kitchen, and Cherie yielded to Brian, eating the bacon and eggs he had prepared for them. She was hungry, she realized, and a good breakfast would help her through the day. She was not too anxious to meet that lawyer again, and the thought of the fingerprint expert sent cold chills down her back.

Still, since Brian wanted her to go and have her fingerprints taken, she would. As she thought this, she reflected that all this seemed far more important to him than to her. Ha! Probably thinking about what a whopping lawyer's fee he would charge.

And yet, if he married her . . .

She smiled at her thoughts and Brian caught that smile. "What's so funny?" he wanted to know.

"Just thinking." She grinned. "But if you really want to know, I was wondering—supposing you ever got around to marrying me—whether I'd have to pay you for your legal services, always assuming I come into the Mannering estate."

A shadow touched his eyes. "We won't worry about that until you are named the heiress."

Just like a lawyer!

She was wearing her cowl-collared maroon dress with the front and back tucking. It was really the only decent thing she had to put on, at least for going to the lawyers' offices. Brian's eyes as they went over her told her that she looked pretty good, but in her own mind, she was not so sure.

If she inherited all that money, the first thing she was

going to do was go clothes-shopping. She would buy as she had never imagined buying. Half a dozen of everything! New dresses, maybe some evening gowns, new slacks, new sweaters, new stockings, undies, and shoes. Yes, she needed a lot of shoes. All she had worn here on the edge of Bayou LaFourche were sneakers.

She wandered out to the car with Brian at her elbow, sort of pushing her along. Not that she was holding back exactly, but she certainly wasn't hurrying. It made no difference to her when they got to New Orleans.

"You seem to be quite a reluctant heiress," he commented as he opened the car door for her. "Any other girl on her way to the Mannering fortune would be running."

She sat still and silent in the seat as he drove along the dirt back roads. No sense in telling him she had been her happiest back there at the cottage. He wouldn't believe her. He was geared to people wanting money or fighting to keep it. Maybe all lawyers were that way.

The day was cloudy, dark. There was a threat of rain in the air, as though the skies themselves were about to weep for her. She felt she might do some weeping on her own, because she had the deep feeling that once she was established as the Mannering heiress, she would never see Brian again.

Phooey! Why did he have to be so high-handed? Why couldn't he be more of a fortune-hunter? She glanced at him, saw how set and hard his face was. Maybe he was thinking along the same lines as she, realizing that once he made sure she got all that money, he was going to lose her.

Didn't the big dope know that he wouldn't lose her, that all he had to do was start to make the offer to marry her and he would be hitched for life? Cherie sighed. Men were so hard to understand sometimes. She sat there and told herself that somehow, someway, she was going to get him to propose.

The rain fell as they drove into New Orleans. It came down in sheets, driven by the wind. Brian slowed the car, driving very carefully.

"Should have thought of an umbrella," he grumbled.

"Won't hurt us to get wet."

He merely grunted at that.

The rain slackened off a little as they were parking. Brian rushed her from the garage across the street and toward the building where Regan, Hennessey, and LeBlanc had their offices. They got spattered with raindrops but not nearly as badly as Brian had feared.

"You all right?" Brian asked, his face etched with worry.

"Sure. What harm can a little rain do me?"

They went up in the elevator, side by side. Then Brian was holding her by the elbow and escorting her into the waiting room. The receptionist nodded at them, smiling, and reached for a phone. A moment later she said, "Mr. LeBlanc will see you now."

She rose to escort them down the hall. The red-carpet treatment, Cherie thought glumly, telling herself that this must surely mean that Charles LeBlanc was almost certain that she was the Mannering heiress. As they came into the lawyer's big office, Cherie came to a dead stop.

She knew one of the men who were seated off to one side of LeBlanc!

Eyes wide, she looked at Brian, who had seen her expression. Instead of speaking, however, he held a chair for her. His eyes seemed almost to warn her not to speak.

"I've gathered the main claimants to the estate here so that we may talk like civilized people," Charles LeBlanc began. "As I've been explaining, it seems right now that your client, Brian, may have the best claim to the Mannering fortune, always assuming, of course, that she passes that fingerprint test."

Brian nodded. "In that case, I suppose we'd better get down to it. Is that fingerprint expert handy?"

"Right down the hall. Wait a moment and I'll have Clara show you to him."

The two cousins sat quietly, their eyes on the floor carpeting. Once in a while one of them would lift his stare to Cherie, studying her. As he did, a look of troubled concern came over his face. She pretended not to notice, but she was very much aware of them, especially the heavyset man, the one with the thick jowls and small, piglike eyes. There was malevolence in those eyes, an almost brutish hate.

A secretary came in; Brian rose and, with Cherie, followed her out into the hall. Cherie leaned closer to Brian, whispered, "That fat guy was the man who followed me home the first day you met me."

Brian stared. "You mean one of the Mannerings?"

"Whoever he is. But I recognized him. There's no mistake about it."

Brian brooded at her side as they entered a room where a man sat behind a table that was spread with inkpads and papers. He rose and smiled at them as the secretary introduced them. As she went out and closed the door, the man pushed a chair forward for Cherie.

"This won't take long. I just want to take the impression of your fingerprints. Now, if you'll let me . . ."

He caught her hand, held it so that one finger was over an inkpad. He put the fingertip on the ink, rotated it gently, then bore the finger to the paper he had set close by. There was silence in the room as he worked, one finger after the other.

When he was done, he lifted the papers, put them to one side. "That's all I need you for. Now comes the hard part. I have to study your prints, compare them to your prints as a child—if those are your prints in that baby book."

Cherie swallowed. "If they are?"

The man chuckled. "Then you're one of the richest women in the world." He shrugged. "If they aren't—you aren't."

"How soon will you know?" Brian asked.

"In a few days. I'll spend all my time on it, I know it's very important."

Brian rose and Cherie followed his example. Brian murmured, "Come on, then. We'll go back and see Charley. I want to ask that so-called cousin of yours if he was following you that day you saw him."

When they returned to the lawyer's office, the two cousins had left. Charles LeBlanc gestured them to chairs, even as Brian began telling him how the heavyset cousin had apparently trailed Cherie home.

Charles LeBlanc frowned when Brian was done. "Odd you should mention that. Luke himself told me something about that."

"Oh?" Cherie leaned forward. "What did he say?"

"He told me much the same thing. Said he had been in New Orleans on that same day, he had noticed you alongside the cathedral railing with your pictures and had been struck by your beauty."

Cherie sneered. "Did he tell you how he stared at me as though he hated me? That he followed me home?"

Charles LeBlanc smiled. "No, he didn't say that. He said that he was quite stricken by your good looks and that he turned and walked away because he didn't want you to be frightened."

"Frightened?"

"That was the word he used. After that he wandered about the French Quarter, then he almost bumped into you again."

"He followed me home!"

The lawyer said soberly, "That's almost impossible to prove."

"That night someone tried to kill me," Cherie said harshly. "It makes sense to me, if not to you. That—that cousin character saw me, recognized how much I looked like Lavinia Mannering, and decided to take no chances. He turned on the gas in my bedroom. I would have died if it hadn't been for Brian."

Charles LeBlanc shrugged. "All guesswork." He leaned forward, studying Cherie's troubled face. "I'm not disputing you, understand. I'm only looking at all this as a lawyer must. What you assume is next to impossible to prove in any court in the country."

Cherie looked at Brian, who nodded. "He's right. You may be right, too, in your belief. But how can we make a case out of it?"

"In the meantime, he may try again!" Cherie looked hard at him. "You were in the car that time when we were almost killed."

"I certainly was. But there again, it may have been a coincidence. Sure, I felt the same way you do about it, I still do. But what can we prove? Absolutely nothing."

Cherie's hands held her little handbag, gripping it tightly. "What you both are saying is, I just have to take my chances. Is that the best two lawyers can do to help me?"

"We could have him bound over to keep the peace," Brian murmured.

"But that wouldn't stop him from hiring someone else to do his dirty work," LeBlanc pointed out.

Cherie got to her feet. "There's no sense in talking, is there? I have to go somewhere and hide until this thing is all settled." There was bitterness in her voice as she added, "The worst part of it all is, I don't care whether I inherit one goddamned cent!"

She stalked from the room and down the hall. Before she was at the door, Brian was beside her, reaching for the knob. "Hey, take it easy," he said. "We're your friends. We want to help you."

"Oh, sure. By getting me killed."

"Nobody wants you to die. Will you take it easy?"

She looked at him through tears glimmering in her eyes. "All r-right. Wha-whatever you say." She swallowed, then muttered. "Let's go to my studio. There are a few things I want to get."

As they came out onto the sidewalk, the rain had stopped and a weak, watery sun was shining down on them. Brian took her arm, saying, "Want to walk? Sometimes it helps, walking. Lets some of the emotions in you ooze away."

Cherie sniffed, but went on walking. Maybe Brian was right. She had to be calm, it didn't help to get overemotional, even if it seemed nobody took her fears very seriously. It was better to enjoy the day, the walk. Brian was with her, and that was all that counted.

They had gone several blocks before she noticed the two men following them. She turned her head to look at the traffic, and the men were there at some little distance. They had stopped as she and Brian stopped, and they stood there staring at them.

Was she going to be attacked again?

She nudged Brian with an elbow, whispered, "Those two men behind us. They keep staring at us, Brian."

He turned, but Cherie noted that the two men did not wait for him to study them, but turned away and walked into a store. Brian asked, "Those two?"

Cherie nodded. "If they come after us—"

Brian grinned. "I wish they would."

Eyes wide, she stared at him. "You do?"

"Sure. I have a red-and-white belt in judo." He chuckled. "There are only two belts higher than that, the red and then the white. Only one man ever got a white belt, and less than twenty the red."

She went on staring at him, even as they walked. "You must be pretty good, then."

"Been at it ever since I was eight years old." He glanced at her. "You know much about judo?"

Cherie shook her head. "I've heard of it, of course, but I never really paid too much attention to it."

"It's an old form of fighting. It started out as jujitsu, some say in China and some in Japan. By the seventeenth century, it was quite well-known. Then it sort of died off. But in the last century a Japanese by the name of Kano opened a jujitsu school—he's the only one entitled to wear the white belt, incidentally—called the Kodokwan.

"President Teddy Roosevelt brought judo—it means 'the gentle way' as contrasted to jujitsu, which means 'the gentle art'—to the United States, and it flourished here. There are a lot of judo schools in the country today."

He talked on as they walked down Canal Street toward Bourbon Street and along that. Cherie noticed that even as he talked he kept looking behind him and on either side. Once he stiffened as a big black car went past them and Cherie asked in alarm, "What is it?"

"I'm not sure. But that black car that just passed us looked familiar."

"Familiar?"

"Don't you remember the car that almost ran us off the road and nearly caused us to have an accident?"

Fear gripped her so hard she could not talk. Finally she managed to blurt, "You think it was the s-same one? I mean the car that just went by?"

"It looked like it. Just walk softly, that's all. Be ready to duck if someone fires at us."

Cherie told herself she was going to fall down. Her knees were too weak, too rubbery to hold her up. She stumbled, but Brian had a grip on her. She turned enormous eyes toward him. "What'll we do?"

"Nothing yet. We're going to your apartment. Let's go."

Panic seized her. "No! We might be walking into a trap!"

"I'd rather walk into a trap when I'm ready for it than to be caught by one when I'm not. Come on, brace up. Just keep walking like a good girl."

She could not help herself. It was as though Brian mesmerized her. She felt her legs and feet moving all the time, but she had no control over them. All she could do was look here and there, seeing danger in every man who walked past or who loitered nearby.

Yet nothing happened. They went along Bourbon Street until they were at Dumaine, and there they headed toward her building. Cherie opened her bag as they went along and got out her key.

Brian said, "Let me have that."

She glanced at him, eyebrows raised.

"They haven't hit us yet," he explained. "They may be in your room, waiting."

She put her hand to her mouth. Her heart came close to stopping as she gasped. "And you're going in? You're going to walk into my place even if those men are in there, waiting for us?"

"I want them to attack me."

He was utterly mad! Off his rocker, completely! She stood and watched as he put the key into the street-level door and opened it. He had to catch her by the arm and draw her into the narrow little hallway after him.

"They won't have guns—I don't think. Knives, maybe." He grinned coldly at her, and Cherie was struck by a facet of this man she loved she had never known before. His eyes were cold, hard.

"And—and you're going up to my room?" she whispered.

"I'd like to get my hands on those two gentlemen. Very much. Don't you see? If I can get hold of one of them, I might be able to make him talk."

"Ha! That'll do us a lot of good if we get killed!"

"We won't get killed. Now, will you come on, please?"

I'm just as nutty as he is, following him like this. But she found her feet were seeking the treads of the stair, going up after him, with the courtyard to her right. Never before had she looked down into that courtyard with such terror in her heart. In a little while she might be dead. So might Brian. She opened her mouth to protest what he was doing, but by that time he had slipped the key into the lock and was turning it, pushing open the door.

As he did, a man hurtled at him, a knife in his hand.

Cherie screamed.

Brian bent, his hand stabbing out to catch the wrist of the hand that held that knife. He bent and swung, his leg coming in front of the other man's legs. The man grunted, his body went sprawling right in front of Cherie.

At the same moment Brian was whirling again, facing the room where another man waited, also armed with a knife. Brian moved into the room—like a leopard hunting its prey, Cherie thought dazedly. The other man rushed him.

Cherie saw Brian move, saw the knife slide past his

turning body, saw Brian seem to turn even as he caught the arm of the knife-wielder, holding that arm against his stomach as he rammed his hand down hard behind the other man's shoulder.

The man screamed. The knife clattered to the floor.

The other man was rising now, eyes on Cherie. He fumbled for the knife he had dropped, then rose with it in a hand. He's coming at me with it. He's going to kill me!

Then the other man seemed to leap forward, banging into the knife-holder's back. It caught him off balance, drove him forward toward the railing. Cherie stepped aside as they both crashed into that railing.

Brian hurled himself at them, feet first. He caught one man in the small of the back, drove him into the other. The railing splintered. For an instant Cherie thought they were going to pitch through the railing and onto the stones of the courtyard below.

At the last moment one of the men grabbed the other, yelled, "Let's get out of here!"

They ran down the narrow porch, not looking behind them.

Life flowed back into Cherie very slowly. She stood on the porch, looking after the men, aware that her heart was coming back to normal, that the blood was flowing more evenly through her veins.

"You all right?" Brian asked.

She nodded dumbly, turning to look at him. "You s-saved m-my life."

He grinned. "Saved my own, too." His eyes were thoughtful as he watched where the men were moving out of sight now, opening the street door and fleeing. Then he looked at the porch floor, where the two knives glinted up at him.

Brian picked the knives up, with his handkerchief. "Proof of an attack, with fingerprints on the handles. We'll turn these over to the police."

Cherie fell into his arms.

15

Brian held her, murmuring words into her thick yellow hair. She nestled against him, knowing deep in her heart that this was where she belonged, in Brian's arms. A deep well of joy bubbled up within her, so that she lost the fear that had gripped her. She inched closer to him, snuggling close.

"It's all over, no need to be alarmed now," he was whispering.

"You were wonderful. Wonderful! If it hadn't been for you . . ."

Her words trailed off as she lifted her face to his. He was so close, his lips were almost on her own. Would the big dope kiss her? Cherie hoped so, fervently.

Brian bent his head. Cherie helped by standing on her tiptoes. Their lips met hungrily, avidly. Cherie felt his arms tighten about her, drawing her even nearer; he almost seemed to want to crush her. And she wanted him to. Her arms were now about his neck, gripping him so that he couldn't draw away. Their tongues touched.

When he drew back, he muttered. "We shouldn't be doing this."

"Why not?" she whispered.

"You're my client!"

"What's that got to do with it?"

She stared up into his eyes, feeling anger mount within her. If he gave her any of that baloney about lawyers and clients, she was going to haul off and swat him one.

"You'll be rich," he said, with misery in his voice. "So rich it scares me."

Cherie opened her eyes wide. "You're scared of money?"

He grinned wryly. "Not of money, exactly, but to marry such a rich woman—Well, I'm not sure about it."

She was beyond speech, but she managed to mutter, "I don't believe this."

She pulled away from him, walked into her apartment, began to throw the few odds and ends she owned into a sort of bundle. She didn't have much, she admitted ruefully, staring at what she owned. No self-respecting thief would even bother with this stuff. But it was hers, and it had some sort of value. To her anyhow.

When she had knotted the ends of the old sheet in which she had piled her things, Brian came and lifted it. Cherie ran her eyes over the little studio-apartment, sighing. When she had first come here, she had been filled with independence and pride. She had been going to make a name for herself in the art world. She had visualized people flocking to her, bringing handfuls of money to get her to do a picture for them.

Bah! The world was full of artists as good as she, even better. Still, it had been fun. She eyed Brian, waiting patiently. He had come like a bombshell into her world and shattered it. Ha! It was up to him to remake that world, to fashion it into a far better place.

She wouldn't let him get away from her, with all his fancy scruples about marrying a rich woman. Somehow, she would think of a way to get him.

"All set?" he asked.

"I guess so." She could not keep the note of sadness out of her voice. This was like putting an end to a period of her life. She was going to turn her back on this part of that life. There would be no going back now.

She trailed after Brian as he walked to the courtyard. If only he showed some sense, if he would just realize that they loved each other instead of being so goddamn noble! Didn't the big goon understand that they were meant for each other? She sneered at his back as she followed it.

When they were in the car and the car was moving, Cherie said, "I never saw those men before, the ones who attacked us."

"They were hired. Hit men, so to speak."

"Who hired them?"

Brian grinned wryly. "Who do you think?"

"My . . . cousins?"

"They have to get rid of you, Cherie. You and you alone stand between them and more than a billion dollars.

It's a high stake they're playing for. In a way I guess I can understand them."

"Oh, sure. I understand them, all right. Kill me, get rich."

"And all you have between you and them is me."

She slithered closer, so that she was resting comfortably against him. "I wouldn't have it any other way."

He glanced down at her a moment before putting his eyes back on the road. "You're crazy, you know that?"

"Mmmmm. I suppose so. Oh, sure. I could hire some bodyguards. Is that what you were going to say? And go hide somewhere with them until this whole damn thing is all over. But I'd rather be with you."

His hand came to grip hers and hold it. Cherie smiled and leaned even closer to him. Like that they drove through New Orleans and out onto the bayou road. The rain had ceased and a weak sun covered the land. By this time Cherie was resting her head on Brian's shoulder and his arm was about her, holding her close.

She drowsed a little, eyes closed, letting thoughts run through her head. It was like going to heaven, returning to that little cottage. It was there her liking for Brian had grown to full-blown love. Or maybe she had fallen in love with him that very first day when he had come offering to pay her for her portrait. Cherie smiled. She hadn't thought of herself as being in love, though. Far from it!

"Did you?" she whispered, half asleep. "Did you fall in love with me that first time you saw me?"

"I tried not to," he muttered.

That brought her up straight, staring at him. "Tried *not* to? Why?"

"If I was right, you were an heiress. You would have more than a billion dollars to your name. You'd never look at a struggling young lawyer."

"Why wouldn't you let me be the judge of what I would and wouldn't do?"

Brian merely shook his head, remaining silent. All of which annoyed Cherie very much. She glowered at him. "You lawyers! Always so careful about what you say!"

"It goes with the trade." He smiled.

"I'd like to bite you," she snapped. "If you weren't driving, I would."

He speeded up, and despite herself, Cherie had to laugh.

She lurched over close to him again, resting her head on his shoulder. "You can be very annoying, you know."

He was silent for a time, then he said, "Only for your own good."

Cherie gritted her teeth.

They came to the cottage when the shadows were growing longer, as a peaceful hush lay all across the bayou world. Cherie sighed at sight of the cottage, telling herself that this was where she'd like to live for always, with Brian. If only . . .

She sighed and got out of the car. A girl with a billion dollars couldn't hide from the world. She had to be out there looking after her money. There would be meetings with lawyers and accountants, with business managers and advisers. Cherie scowled. What did she know about such things?

Still! Brian would know.

"I'll fix dinner," she told him as they walked to the cottage, Brian carrying her things wrapped in the sheet. "You hungry?"

"Not very. How about club sandwiches and coffee?"

She shrugged, telling herself that she had no appetite, either. As far as she was concerned, they could skip dinner and just sit out here in the twilight and look at the stars, when they came out. It would be romantic. But Brian, being a man, would want his meal. A creature of habit, that's all he was.

Yet as she cooked bacon and he sliced tomatoes, she admitted that there was a teeny part of her which would not reject a few bites of a club sandwich and a couple of cups of hot coffee. As a matter of fact, if she could be sure that Brian would pull her into a bedroom with him after they ate, she might get mighty hungry.

They carried their trays outside and sat and ate as the world darkened around them. Brian was being very quiet, he hardly opened his mouth. Since she did not feel much like talking, only the faint sounds from the bayou came to disturb the silence. Cherie heard a fish jump and splash in the water, she heard the creaking of a frog, the bellow of an alligator, far away.

"Guess we'd better get to sleep," Brian muttered after a long time. "We've had an active day."

There went her hopes of an even more active night. Oh, well. Short of slugging the guy and forcing him into her bed, there wasn't much she could do about it. Cherie sighed and nodded.

But when she was between her sheets and staring wide-eyed at the darkened ceiling above her, she told herself that being a rich heiress wasn't all it was cracked up to be. Even if she had that billion dollars in bed with her, it wouldn't tempt Brian Cutler. He was above temptation. Cherie fell asleep with the sneer on her mouth.

"Rise and shine!"

The words disturbed a very nice dream she had been having about Brian Cutler. They were standing in a church, about to be married. Brian had been about to slip the ring on her finger.

Cherie wriggled under the covers. "Go away!"

"Coffee's on."

Ha! He knew what he could do with his coffee. "I'm sleepy."

He was kneeling on the bed now and bending over her. Cherie burrowed deeper under the covers. Then he was kissing her cheek, sliding his lips down toward the corner of her mouth. Well, now. This was something. Almost lazily, she began to turn over.

But as she did, he got off the bed and stood there grinning down at her. "Better get up and dress. We're going swimming today and maybe do a little clamming on the way."

Cherie scowled and threw back the covers. Brian made a little sound, and too late she realized she was wearing that threadbare shortie nightgown. She sniffed. Let the dope look. He wouldn't do anything about it.

"It is warm," she said. "It'll be a good day for a swim. As a matter of fact, I think I'll have breakfast in this old thing I'm wearing. It's cool enough."

Cool? It was practically nonexistent. All the better. Let the guy stare—and realize what he was passing up. Head high, she walked past him.

Brian came after her, and it seemed to Cherie that his footsteps were a little uncertain. She grinned. Serve him right.

He had cooked her bacon and eggs. She ate across from him to make certain that he had to see her in that nightie. His eyes touched her, slid away several times. But always they came back. Cherie gloated deep inside her. Let's see how noble he really is.

Whey they were done and the dishes washed and dried, Cherie murmured, "I'll go put on my swimsuit."

There wasn't very much to that, either, she reflected.

Brian rowed the pirogue through the bayou waters with Cherie sitting ahead of him in the back of the boat. She leaned back on her hands, letting the sun warm her. Brian made easy going with the oars, as long as he stared away from her. But as soon as his stare drifted over her, he pulled a crab, spraying water with an oar.

"Having trouble?" she asked sweetly.

He merely grunted, but he pulled harder on the oars after that and steadfastly refused to look at her. Cherie eyed him speculatively. She was going to break through that wall of seeming indifference that he had erected between them. She was going to do it very soon, too.

She walked ahead of him when they came to the grassy lands surrounding their little lake, letting her hips swing indolently. If he didn't want to look, he didn't have to. What difference did it make? But he was a man, and Cherie would have bet those billion dollars that he was eyeing her up and down, all right.

They waded in and swam. When they came to the middle of the little lake, Cherie cried out. Instantly Brian swam to her, asking, "What is it? What's wrong?"

"I thought I felt something under the water!"

"Here, lean on me."

She wrapped her arms about him and plastered her wet body to his. He had to put an arm around her, and Cherie pressed more closely. "It's so good to be here with you to protect me, Brian," she murmured. "You give me such a feeling of confidence."

"I'm not doing anything," he murmured deprecatingly.

Ha! He could say that again. Her eyes looked up at him worshipfully. "But you are. Just being near you is enough. Just having you hold me like this is making me feel good about everything."

This was when he should have kissed her and protested his undying love. But the guy seemed to slip away from her—though he still had hold of her arm—and said, "We'd better be getting back. I don't want you catching a chill."

He was the one with a chill. Cherie muttered under her breath, but she swam back with him to the grassland. They baked awhile under the sun, which dried them, and then Brian rose to his feet. "Better be going now. I want to do a little clamming."

Cherie sat and scowled while he worked at getting them some clams for dinner. She had only one hope where Brian was concerned. Maybe she would not inherit all that money. In that case he might break down and ask her to marry him.

I'd marry him, all right, even if it meant half-starving for the rest of my life. Who needs money, anyhow?

He rowed back in the early afternoon with a good catch of clams on the floorboards of the pirogue. Cherie sat with chin on fist, eyeing him sulkily, trying to think of some way she could get him to admit that he loved her, that he couldn't live without her. She could think of nothing.

She made the sauce while he opened the clams. She had taken off the swimsuit and put on an almost equally negligible sunsuit she had brought from the apartment yesterday. She padded about on bare feet, too.

They ate in the early evening, munching on clams and the clam chowder Cherie had made. Cherie watched him eat heartily, telling herself that he was going to waste all that energy he was absorbing by sleeping alone. She wondered what excuse he was going to give.

"All that sun today made me sort of sleepy," he said at last.

"Of course." She smiled sweetly. Last night he had said that they had had too much excitement or something equally nonsensical. What she ought to do was let him get into bed, then crawl in with him. She grinned at the idea.

Tomorrow night, maybe. Not tonight. She wanted to lull him into a sense of security. It would be false, but what the heck. She rose from the table and began gathering dishes.

"Get a good night's sleep," she told him as he walked toward his bedroom.

"You, too." He nodded.

Cherie snarled as his door closed behind him. She moved into her room and slammed her door hard. It made a loud noise. She hoped he had heard it. Even more important, she hoped he understood it.

She woke early next morning, lying under the covers and listening for Brian. There was no sound in the cottage. Had he overslept? Cherie grinned. If he had, she would walk into his room and wake him with a kiss. However, unlike him, she would not step back when he woke up. She would slip under the sheets with him. Then she would see how strong he was.

She giggled as she ran to the door and yanked it open. To her surprise, Brian was standing in the middle of the living room with a rifle in his hands. As she came out, he held a finger to his lips and whispered. "Don't say a word."

Cherie gulped. There was something about him—a grimness—that frightened her. She tiptoed close. "What is it?"

"I heard a car a little while ago. It stopped a good distance away. Then there was only silence."

She stared at him. "But—"

"Have you forgotten those men the other day? They may be outside, waiting for us to come out."

"They're *here?*" she wailed.

"Stay down. Lie on the floor. Go on!"

She did what he said, watching as he moved toward the door, turning the knob and opening it. Nothing happened. Cherie watched as Brian moved toward a window and peered out. She waited for several minutes, then stood up.

As she did, something whistled past her ear.

Brian turned then, seeing her standing. His face went white. "Get down," he bellowed, "away from the door."

He ran then, toward the door. He flung himself out into the sunlight, gun up. Cherie saw him hit the ground and roll. She saw dirt spring up where a bullet landed. Brian had the gun to his shoulder and was firing.

"Oh, dear God," she whimpered and lay flat.

This could not be. In this day and age, men did not shoot to kill each other here in Louisiana. Ha! What a joke that was! Men were doing that very thing. Cherie looked around her for another gun, but decided that since she did not know how to handle guns, she had better leave the shooting to Brian. He seemed to be doing all right.

He was up and running, moving toward the trees.

From somewhere in those trees, a rifle sounded. Brian staggered, fell flat—and Cherie screamed. Her world stopped right then and there. Nothing existed but the fact that Brian was hurt. Shot! Maybe—*dead!*

At a stumbling run, she moved toward him, only to see him roll over, throw the rifle to his shoulder, and fire. From somewhere—she could not estimate distance in her excited state—a man cried out thickly. There was the sound of someone falling onto twigs and underbrush.

Then there was a silence.

Brian turned his head, saw her. His hand motioned vigorously and Cherie realized that she was standing out there on the lawn, fully visible to anyone who cared to look. She dropped to the ground even as there was the sound of another rifle firing. Something brushed her pajama bottoms. She hit the ground and lay there, realizing that one of those men had shot at her.

If she did not move, he would think her dead.

Heart thudding, she made herself remain still, not even raising her head to look at Brian, who was shooting again. Faintly, now, she could hear the sound of footsteps running. Then there was only silence.

No. She could hear a car motor start up, far away. The motor roared, grew louder, then settled to a drone that died away. Whoever had shot at them was fleeing. Was it safe now to raise her head, to peer around?

Better wait awhile. She continued to lie quiet until she heard footsteps approaching. Brian? Or—one of the killers? But the killers had fled away, hadn't they? Someone had gone, she was sure of that.

"Cherie? Oh, dear God . . ."

That was Brian. She was about to rise and tell him she was all right when she felt him kneel beside her and put his hands on her shoulders.

He was lifting her, taking her in his arms, holding her. He was sobbing, too, very softly. Cherie opened her mouth to let him know she was unharmed when an inner voice whispered to her that it might be better to let the guy worry just a little.

"My darling, my darling," he was whispering. "I'll never forgive myself. Oh, Cherie! I loved you so much. So much! This is all my fault. All my fault."

He was crushing her to him, kissing her throat, her cheeks. This was so pleasant that Cherie did not want to break the spell by talking. Let him think her dead. That way he could go on telling her how much he loved her without getting any guilt feelings or whatever else it was that kept him mum while she was alive and healthy.

It was hard, though, not to embrace him, just to lie here and let him pour out his heart to her. Besides, she had to breathe. It wasn't easy, holding her breath and pretending to be dead. Finally she drew in a breath of air.

Brian eased the grip he held on her, staring down at her with wide eyes. "You're alive!" he yelled.

No sense in trying to fool him anymore. Cherie opened her eyes and peered up at him. Maybe he saw the laughter in her eyes, because he began to scowl.

"Are you hurt?" he asked gruffly.

"No, I'm fine. And I'm glad you love me so much."

"Better forget I said that."

"Why? Are you scared of me?"

"No, I'm not scared. But I didn't want you getting hurt. I'd be a fine lawyer if I went and let you get shot while you were in my company, wouldn't I?"

"You—you—" The anger rose up inside her in a great tide. She pushed him back, got to her feet. Her cheeks were red, her eyes flared. Her hands were clenched into little fists. "You're a coward, Brian Cutler, that's what you are! A coward! You love me, but you're afraid to admit it."

"You may be right." He sighed.

She kicked his shin, hard. Then she swung a fist for his face.

Her fist landed hard on his cheek. Brian didn't even raise his hand to protect himself. He just stood there, misery in his eyes. Cherie felt like a heel.

Then a change came over him, even as he stared down into her eyes. His arms lifted, caught her. He jerked her forward against him and began kissing her. They were hard, furious kisses, too, kisses that bruised her lips, crushing them. Cherie felt herself being crushed to his chest, his loins, his thighs. It was a great feeling, she told herself. Brian should lose control more often.

"I love you," he was whispering. "Can't you get that through your silly little skull? I worship you, I adore the ground you walk on. I love your toes, your tiny feet, those lovely legs, your hips . . ."

He went on kissing her hungrily, fiercely. Cherie reveled in it, kissing him back just as wildly as he was kissing her. Much more of this and they were going to lose control.

Then, of course, he came to his senses and began to push her back and away. "Forget what I was babbling," he growled. "I had no right to do that or to say what I did."

Was there ever such a man? How did a girl handle

somebody like this? Cherie fought hard not to be angry with him. The poor guy didn't know whether he was coming or going.

She stepped back, said, "I think you hit one of the men, didn't you?"

Slightly dazed, he stared down at her. "Of course! I heard him cry out. Come on, let's go see. No! You'd better wait here. He may be only slightly wounded."

Cherie tilted her chin. She let him turn and walk away, then she went after him. She might be able to help him if that wounded man showed fight.

They came up on him where he lay facedown in a clump of bushes. His rifle was half a dozen feet away, and he was groaning. Cherie could see the blood on his knee and on the ground. He was in no mood to fight, she knew at once.

16

Brian stepped close to the man, rifle at the alert. Cherie ran around and picked up the fallen rifle, aiming it at the man on the ground. If he had a handgun on him and threatened Brian, she was going to shoot.

The man went on groaning.

Brian said, "Don't make a move."

"How can I move? You shot me through the knee. Do you know how much that hurts?"

Brian knelt, ran his hand over the man to make certain he had no hidden gun on him. Then he handed Cherie his gun, bent, and turned the man over, helping him to his one good leg. "Can you hop?" he asked.

They got the man into the cottage, where Brian cut away his trouser leg and began to doctor him. "Lucky for you the bullet went through. Otherwise, I'd have to probe for it."

The man grunted. He was young, with long brown hair and a stubble beard. His clothes were old, mended, and worn. His face was pale with pain, but he seemed appreciative of what Brian was doing for him. When he was done, Brian sat back on his heels.

"I have to get you to a doctor. Otherwise, you might lose that leg. But before I do, I want you to talk."

The man glared at him. "Talk about what?"

"Who paid you to try and kill Cherie Marsan?"

The man sneered. "Think I'll tell?"

Brian rose to his feet and shrugged. "Okay. Don't talk. Just get out."

"You can't mean that! I'll never make it to a town, to another house. I'll die out there."

Brian grinned. "Sure you will, but why should I care? This is a war you're in, man. You against us. Why should I care whether you live or die?"

The other man thought about that a moment. Then he

shrugged. "What the hell! I don't owe them guys anything. You want to know who's paying for us to kill that girl? I'll tell you. Two men. Their names are Mannering. Luke and Norris Mannering."

Cherie gasped. Her cousins! Those two men who were in the lawyer's office when she had gone to have her fingerprints taken! Her eyes sought out Brian, who was nodding, saying, "You willing to make a deposition to that effect? And sign it?"

"Why not? What do I owe them? Sure, I'll sign."

Brian hesitated, then asked, "How did you find us?"

Jackie Ben Fruman grinned. "We checked deeds in the Hall of Records and learned that you and your brother had a place out here on the bayou." He shrugged. "We drove out here, asked a question or two, and drove here. It wasn't too hard."

Brian turned away, sought out pen and paper. He began to write. The man with the bandaged knee stared at him, then yelled, "Hey! You going to let me die while you write letters?"

"This is a confession. You're going to sign it, mister— before I take you to any doctor. Relax. You won't die."

When they were finished and the man had set his signature to the paper, Brian helped him out to the Granada. He also tied his hands around behind his back. When he protested, Brian said, "I wouldn't put it past you to try to knock me out and take my car. I'm taking no chances."

Cherie said, "Give me a gun, Brian. If he makes one move, I'll shoot him."

"Easy, lady. I'm not going to make any moves."

"Why should I take it easy? You were trying to kill me, weren't you?" She grinned. "I can always claim you lunged against the rifle and made it go off, right?"

The man paled as he felt Cherie's eyes boring into him. He did not trust this dame, no way. If he had entertained any ideas about trying to escape, he forgot them. Better to stay alive and serve time than be a dead hero.

They drove to the local hospital, and while a doctor was looking at Jackie Ben Fruman's wounded knee, Brian phoned the local chief of police. When he was done, he turned to Cherie, said, "We'll have to wait around and tell him what happened."

She nodded, knowing Brian was going to tell her more. "Then we're going back to New Orleans and lay a complaint against your two cousins. I want them picked up and charged. Then we'll go see Charley LeBlanc."

"Oh?"

"I want to know about that fingerprint test. Don't you?"

Cherie shrugged. She would much rather go back to the cottage with Brian than anywhere else. But she realized that when he got in one of these lawyerish moods, there was nothing to do but go along with him.

It was a little more than two hours before the chief of police let them go, promising that Jackie Ben Fruman would be behind bars just as soon as the hospital let him go. The chief grinned coldly, assuring Brian that he would not escape.

They had to return to the cottage for Cherie to change into a dress. If she were to wear her sunsuit in New Orleans, she was afraid she might be arrested for public indecency. It was fine to wear it around where only Brian would see her in it, but there were limits. At the same time, Brian donned a business suit, with shirt and tie.

The drive into New Orleans was pleasant. They stopped on the way for a sandwich and coffee, and it was midafternoon by the time they were ushered into Charles LeBlanc's office. He rose to his feet at sight of them and came to hold a chair for Cherie.

"Sit here, Miss Mannering, if you please."

Cherie eyed him. "Miss Mannering?"

The lawyer smiled, nodded. "Your fingerprints matched. No doubt about it. You stand to inherit the whole estate. It's worth well over a billion dollars."

She looked at Brian. He had also taken a chair and was staring out the window, his face inscrutable. Ha! She knew what he was thinking, all right. Now that she was rich, that was the end of their little romance. He was only a poor, struggling lawyer, he had nothing to offer her. Phooey on all that!

"Well," she said. "So that's that. What do I do now?"

Charles LeBlanc laughed. "Nothing at all. Everything will be taken care of. We'll submit all the papers to the surrogate. Oh, there may be a paper or two for you to sign, but not to worry. It will all be taken care of." He glanced at Brian. "I assume Brian here is still your lawyer?"

"Of course."

"Then I'll deal with him." The lawyer sat at ease, hands together on his desktop. "You don't have to do a thing."

In other words, everything will be handed over to me on a golden platter. Everything—except the one thing I really want.

Charles LeBlanc looked at her, puzzled. "You don't seem to care very much, I must say. I expected you to jump up and down in delight."

Cherie shrugged. "Money doesn't mean all that much to me, frankly. It can't buy what isn't for sale."

LeBlanc looked even more puzzled, but Brian shot her a glance. *He knows what I'm talking about!*

Brian was saying, leaning forward and handing over the signed confession, "Here's something I want you to see, Charley. I want the district attorney working on this right away. I'm going to go see him myself, but I would appreciate a few words from you."

LeBlanc read over the confession, his face paling. When he was done, he laid it flat on his desk blotter, then said, "Of course. I want you to know I knew absolutely nothing about this."

Brian grinned and waved a hand. The lawyer went on, "I'll call the district attorney at once and hold this for him. The two Mannerings will be arrested before nightfall, charged with attempted murder." He smiled weakly and looked at Cherie. "You have nothing more to worry about, Miss Mannering. Those cousins of yours will be behind bars as soon as they are apprehended."

· He turned to some papers on his desk, smiling at Cherie. "I have the fingerprint-test results, Miss Mannering. As Brian suspected, they show that you are, indeed, Clarissa Theresa Mannering. There's no doubt about it, none at all. And so—my congratulations."

He turned and took a key ring from his desk. "You might as well have these. They're the keys to Oak Haven. It will be your home from now on, I assume."

Cherie took the keys, turning them over and over in her fingers. Oak Haven meant nothing to her, unless Brian were there to share it with her. She felt tears start up in her eyes and felt miserable.

Brian was getting to his feet, reaching out to shake Charles LeBlanc's hand. "We can work on the legal details later, Charley. I'd like to drive Miss Mannering over to Oak Haven right now."

"Go ahead. I'll phone the D.A. and talk to him." Le-
Blanc looked at Cherie. "Don't worry anymore, Miss
Mannering. Everything will be smooth sailing for you
from now on."

Oh, sure. I'm a poor little rich girl. Phooey!

She padded out after Brian, stood quietly with him waiting for the elevator. Only when they were on the street,
did she speak.

"Do I have to go to Oak Haven?" she asked meekly.

Brian smiled. "You own it, Cherie. It's all yours. So are
those stocks and bonds, all the ships and oil wells and everything else. You must have half a million or more in
cash in the banks. I'm not sure about the exact figures."

She slid into the car seat and waited as Brian started the
car. She sat and thought and got nowhere. Brian was going to abandon her, leave her in that huge mausoleum all
by herself. Tears came into her eyes and she blinked them
away.

Weakly she asked, "How will I get around without you
to drive me?"

"Hey, you own a Rolls-Royce, a Jaguar roadster, a
Mercedes. So you don't know how to drive. Hire some-
body to teach you. Then you can go anywhere you want.
Buy anything you want, too."

None of that impressed her. All she wanted was Brian.

After a time, she asked, "What are you going to do?"

"Go back to my law practice. I've neglected it sadly of
late. Oh, yeah. I'll probably send you a bill one of these
days."

"Aren't you going to be my lawyer any longer?"

"Why, sure. Charley will hand over the estate to me,
once it's been settled. I'll be out to see you, ask your advice about what you want to do, that sort of thing."

They pulled up before the big house. There were no visitors today, Cherie saw. Charles LeBlanc had probably
closed the house down just as soon as he knew that she
was the owner. It was all hers. She stared at the mansion
almost with hate. If it weren't for her having inherited it,
Brian would have asked her to marry him.

He got out of the car, opened her door, walked with her
to the door, and opened it for her. Then he handed her
the keys.

"These are yours now. I'll be running along."

"Brian—don't go."

"Cherie, I have a living to make."

He squeezed her hand, turning on a heel, and walked away. She stood in the open doorway, watching him go. Her heart felt like lead. She wanted to die!

What was there to live for?

Cherie wandered about the house, scowling at the painting of Lavinia Mannering, discovering that there was no food in the several refrigerators she found in the kitchen and the cellar. Good. Maybe she would starve to death. Then Brian Cutler would be sorry!

Then she discovered that the telephone worked.

The first thing she had to do was order some food. Then she needed somebody to take care of the house. After that, she would call up somebody to teach her how to drive. She sat beside the telephone and started making notes, and began to feel a little better.

Two weeks went by, during which Cherie kept very busy. She hired servants, she bought food, she took lessons in how to drive a car. Now that she had a learner's permit and had taken a couple of lessons, she felt much better about things. Twice she had telephoned the law offices Brian shared with his brother, but Brian had not been there. The receptionist had told her that Brian had not been in for several days.

She was walking about the grounds one morning when a big Continental moved up the drive. To her surprise, Cara Slagle got out and began walking toward her. As she drew closer, Cherie saw that she was smiling weakly.

"I suppose you're wondering what I'm doing here," Cara began. "I heard the news about your turning out to be the heiress of old Josiah Mannering and I've been arguing with myself ever since about whether I ought to come over here and say hello or not."

Cherie smiled. "Why not? What difference does it make?"

Cara eyed her closely. She sighed. "You probably think I have some nerve. Well, maybe I do. Anyhow, I've come to see the light. I'm not interested in Brian Cutler anymore."

"He doesn't belong to me," Cherie snapped tartly.

"Oh, but he does. Why do you think he's in hiding?"

"I didn't know he was."

Cara sniffed. "Ran away just as soon as you came into your inheritance. His brother told me he's been pretty hard hit. By you, that is. He won't go back to the office. He just mopes around."

"Where?" The word shot from Cherie like a bullet from the gun.

"At that cottage of his. He's gone native. Goes out and gets his own food, won't come into town. He's become a hermit."

Cherie knew a wild excitement. Maybe Brian felt as miserable as she did. In that case, it was up to her to go out and talk some sense into him. By a sheer effort of will, she controlled herself.

"Why not come in and have a cup of coffee?" she offered. "We really ought to get to know each other." Cherie scowled. "To be honest with you, I feel like a fish out of water. I'm not used to being rich."

Cara laughed. "It isn't hard getting used to." She paused and studied Cherie, then held out her hand. "Friends?"

Cherie nodded and caught her hand, squeezing it. "I need advice. You game for that coffee?"

"I'm dying for it."

They had coffee served to them by a maid in the breakfast room. Over it, they began to chat. Cherie admitted that she needed clothes, but didn't know where to shop. All the places she had bought clothes in the past were now behind her. She had the feeling that she ought to buy in the better stores, but was afraid.

"Pooh!" Cara exclaimed, leaning back, eyes shining. "That's the easiest part of it. You come with me and bring your checkbook—or better yet, establish charge accounts. The big stores will fall all over themselves opening credit for Clarissa Mannering."

"Wait until I change."

They spent the day buying clothes. They lunched together, talking and laughing.

Cara said, "Brian's too noble for his own good. Somehow you've got to make him understand that he means more to you than all your money."

Cherie scowled. "Sure. But how?"

Cara reached across the table and patted her hand. "You'll think of a way, my dear. Never fear."

Cherie wasn't so sure. She remembered how Brian had repulsed her when he knew she was the heiress to the Mannering fortune. What reason did he have for changing now? He would still be the same old Brian. On the other hand, he might have changed his mind, at least a little.

She had to find out.

Next morning she slid into her old, worn sunsuit, throwing a light coat over it, then ran out to the Jaguar roadster. She did not have her license yet, but she had her learner's permit. It would have to do. She started the car, drove slowly out the drive and just as slowly along the road that would take her, eventually, to the dirt track that wound through bayou land to Brian's cottage.

It was a warm morning, the sun was high overhead, there was not a cloud in the sky. She wondered as she drove, what Brian might be doing. Was he out clamming? Off swimming in that little lake? No matter. She would wait for him if he wasn't at the cottage.

Her chin was set determinedly.

As she came to the clearing where the cottage was located, she saw the Granada. He was here, then. Her heart began to bang as she climbed out of the Jaguar and approached the house. She didn't bother to knock, she opened the door and walked in.

Brian was not in the house. Cherie scowled, then ran to the front door and out onto the lawn. The pirogue was there, too. Where, then, was Brian?

As she turned, irresolute, movement out of the corner of her eyes caught her attention. Someone was walking down the road toward the cottage. Cherie ran. Now she could see it was Brian. He was wandering along, hands thrust deep in his pockets, a lost expression on his face. From time to time, he sighed.

Cherie waited until he was almost on the lawn. Then he looked up and saw the Jaguar, turned as if to flee.

"Don't you dare, Brian Cutler!"

He swung about, face flushing. "Don't what?" he muttered.

"Don't you dare run away from me!"

She dropped the coat, let it pool at her feet. Then she moved toward him, wearing the threadbare sunsuit. His eyes went all over her, she noted. Hmmm. That was a good sign.

"What do you want?" he asked. "You aren't having any trouble, are you?"

She was close to him now. "Of course I'm having trouble. Do you think it's fun to be cooped up in that mausoleum of a mansion all by myself? I'd sooner be back on Dumaine Street!"

He looked bewildered. "But you're rich!"

"Rich! Rich! Do you think money is everything?" She hesitated, then asked, "Aren't you going to ask me in for a cup of coffee, even?"

"Oh. Sure. Come on."

In the kitchen she moved toward the coffee tin and ladled out the coffee. Brian had gone to the cupboard for two cups and saucers. It seemed to Cherie that his step was lighter, he seemed to have lost his gloomy look. Well, that was encouraging, anyhow.

"Have you missed me?" she asked softly.

"A little. I've—er—gotten used to having you around."

"You haven't been working."

He shrugged. "I haven't felt like it."

"You're becoming a bum."

He nodded gloomily. Cherie turned to the stove, poured the coffee, then sat down. "While I was shopping yesterday, I bought something for you," she said.

"Oh? What?"

"A wedding ring." She added airily. "I bought one for myself, too. They match."

He was shaking his head while she reached into the pocket of the sunsuit. "Here they are." She pushed the two little black boxes across the table toward him.

Brian looked at them for a long moment. Then he reached out and opened them, staring down at the brilliant diamonds.

"One for you, one for me," she said softly.

He looked into her eyes then. He said slowly, "I'm not rich enough for you. Oh, I've done pretty well at my law practice. But—"

"The way you conduct it, you're going to have nothing left in a few weeks. You're putting all the burden on your brother."

Brian nodded gloomily while she sipped her coffee, resisting the urge to kick his shin. Did she have to go down on her knees and beg him to marry her? Anger began to rise up inside her. Then tears came into her eyes and she began to sob.

He looked at her in dismay. "Hay, listen. Please don't cry. I love you, you know that!"

"Th-then why d-don't you sh-show it?"

The tears came faster now, running down her cheeks. Brian leaped to his feet, ran around to her side of the table, knelt down beside her.

Somehow, she was in his arms and crying more loudly than ever. Almost wailing, a corner of her mind told her. Brian hugged her, kissed her, held her tightly.

"For Pete's sake, will you stop crying!"

"Wh-why sh-should I? You s-say you l-love me and you won't ma-ma-marry me!"

Suddenly he was smiling, holding her by the shoulders and pushing her back so he could look into her tear-wet face. "You know something, Cherie? I'm a nut. No, not a nut. A damn fool!"

She nodded, half-laughing through her tears. "You certainly are."

"Here I've been moping around, not caring whether I lived or died, and all the time happiness was just waiting for me."

"Sure it is." She smiled. She leaned forward and kissed him very gently. "You have plenty of money. You haven't even sent me a bill for legal services. I figure it ought to amount to about a million dollars, if not more."

"No. Not that much!"

"Yes, that much. I insist!"

Almost dreamily he said, "I could support even you on a million dollars."

"I'm not that expensive a wife."

"Oh, yes, you are. I'd want you to have the best of everything. But I'd want to buy it for you."

"Suppose I don't want anything but you?"

His laughter rang out. "I was just thinking the same thing. You're all I want."

"I come cheap. All it takes is a wedding license."

He shook his head. "No. You're somebody now. You're a member of society. The wedding will have to be a big one. There'll be important people to invite, to be fed and entertained."

"But—"

He smiled down into her eyes. "You are Clarissa Theresa Mannering now. You aren't just my Cherie anymore."

Cherie pouted. "I don't want to be Clarissa Theresa Mannering."

"You'll only be that to the world. You'll always be Cherie to me."

An idea came to her. Thoughtfully, she asked, "When will we be married?"

"In a month, about. That'll be time enough for everything to be done as it should."

"We'll start first thing in the morning," Cherie said decisively.

Brian blinked his surprise. "In the morning?"

Cherie grinned wickedly. "Remember how you told me that you'd like to take your girl out to the lake and stay there overnight in a tent?"

"Sure. But—"

"Well? Do you have a tent?"

"Of course I do."

"What are we waiting for, then?" She laughed.

They ran together out into the sunlight, hand in hand.

SIGNET Double Romances for the Price of One!

☐ **SIGNET DOUBLE ROMANCE—FOLLOW THE HEART** by Heather Sinclair and **FOR THE LOVE OF A STRANGER** by Heather Sinclair. (#J8363—$1.95)*

☐ **SIGNET DOUBLE ROMANCE—IT HAPPENED IN SPAIN** by Ivy Valdes and **CRISTINA'S FANTASY** by Ivy Valdes. (#E7983—$1.75)

☐ **SIGNET DOUBLE ROMANCE—GIFT FROM A STRANGER** by Ivy Valdes and **OVER MY SHOULDER** by Ivy Valdes. (#E8181—$1.75)

☐ **SIGNET DOUBLE ROMANCE—SHEILA'S DILEMMA** by Ivy Valdes and **THE INTRUSION** by Elizabeth McCrae. (#W7440—$1.50)†

☐ **SIGNET DOUBLE ROMANCE—THE DAWN OF LOVE** by Teri Lester and **TANIA** by Teri Lester. (#E7804—$1.75)

☐ **SIGNET DOUBLE ROMANCE—A CONFLICT OF WOMEN** by Emma Darby and **HAVEN OF PEACE** by I. Torr. (#W7370—$1.50)

☐ **SIGNET DOUBLE ROMANCE—RETURN TO LOVE** by Peggy Gaddis and **ENCHANTED SPRING** by Peggy Gaddis. (#W7158—$1.50)

☐ **SIGNET DOUBLE ROMANCE—SECRET HONEYMOON** by Peggy Gaddis and **HANDFUL OF MIRACLES** by Marion Naismith. (#Y6761—$1.25)

* Price slightly higher in Canada
† Not available in Canada

Buy them at your local
bookstore or use coupon
on next page for ordering.

Ⓢ

Big Bestsellers from SIGNET

SIGNET Books by Glenna Finley

* Price slightly higher in Canada

Buy them at your local
bookstore or use coupon
on next page for ordering.